"Are you prepared to tell me the truth now?"

Olivia looked more beautiful than ever. "There's one important thing you should know." Ford pulled her into his arms and kissed her slowly. She tasted exotic and so hot....

"Stop!" Breathing heavily, she backed across the room, wishing she weren't so attracted to a man she couldn't trust. After all, she'd seen him steal an amulet from the museum. "You know I'm concerned about Charlie. Why are you lying to me?"

"Let me handle it my own way," Ford said, still tasting her lips on his.

Olivia gasped. "You know where my brother is, don't you?"

Ford scrutinized her from beneath his hooded eyes. "Maybe."

Dear Readers,

Since we were young we have wanted to see the world—to visit all the exotic places we saw in films and read about in books. *Night of the Nile* comes from an unbelievable adventure cruise up the Nile River we took a year ago. It exceeded even our high expectations. The pyramids that had fascinated us from youth, the treasure that Tut's tour of the United States had whetted our appetites for, the mystery, the wonder, cannot be described. We hope Olivia and Ford's pursuit of the ancient mysteries will convey to you our own sense of marvel about this international treasure trove.

We hope that you will enjoy adventuring with us to our "Ports of Call" and that love fills your life with happiness.

Love,

Lynn Leslie

Night of the Nile

Lynn Leslie

Harlequin Books

TORONTO • NEW YORK • LONDON
AMSTERDAM • PARIS • SYDNEY • HAMBURG
STOCKHOLM • ATHENS • TOKYO • MILAN
MADRID • WARSAW • BUDAPEST • AUCKLAND

To Pat Sims and Lynda Silverman—
Let's go back to Egypt and experience the wonder all over again! Our apologies to serious Egyptologists for taking some slight liberties with the Osiris-Isis Legend. We know they will understand that some things are simply too private to mention.

ISBN 0-373-22287-4

NIGHT OF THE NILE

This edition published by arrangement with Harlequin Enterprises B. V.

Printed in U.S.A.

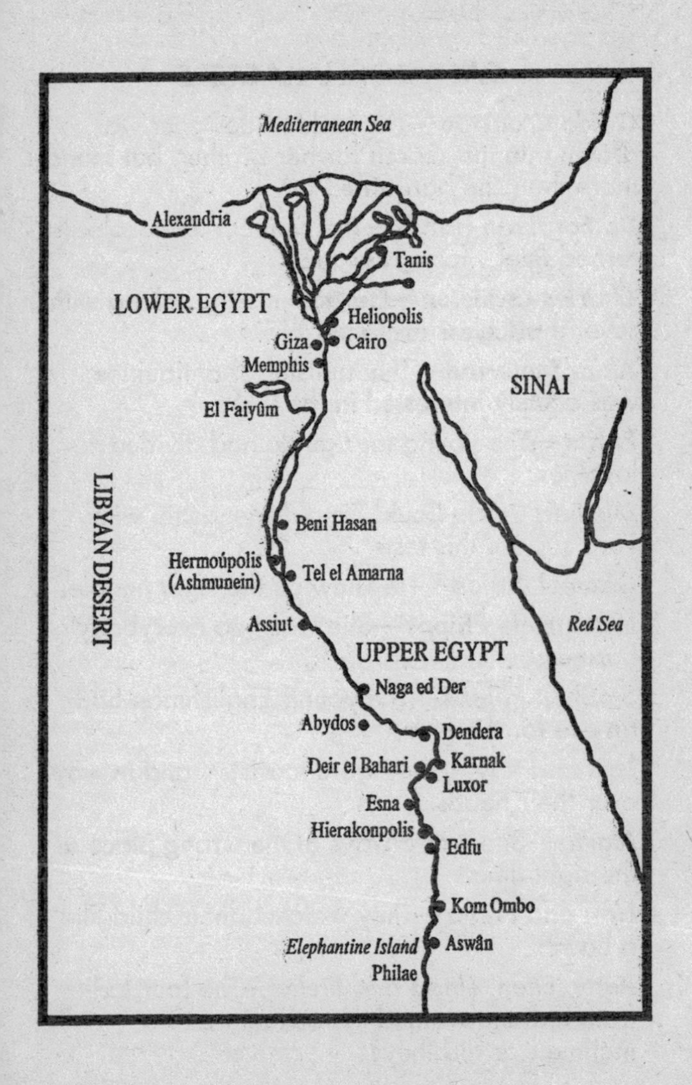

Mediterranean Sea
Alexandria
Tanis
LOWER EGYPT
Heliopolis
Giza
Cairo
Memphis
El Faiyûm
SINAI
LIBYAN DESERT
Beni Hasan
Hermoúpolis
(Ashmunein)
Tel el Amarna
Assiut
Red Sea
UPPER EGYPT
Naga ed Der
Abydos
Dendera
Deir el Bahari
Karnak
Luxor
Esna
Hierakonpolis
Edfu
Kom Ombo
Elephantine Island
Aswân
Philae

CAST OF CHARACTERS

Olivia Cranston—The fashion designer was drawn into the search for her brother, but found more than she bargained for.

Dr. Fordham Harris—The eminent archaeologist turned thief...for a reason.

Charles Cranston—He was missing, along with several priceless artifacts.

Akim Tamarian—The minister of antiquities was acutely interested in the thefts.

Farita—The young tour guide had divided loyalties.

Mustafa Bey—Could his old friendship with Ford survive this test?

Gameel Mujod—He knew all the right people.

Irmentrude Phipps—She was into everybody's business.

Stephen Phipps—The young Englishman had an eye for the girls.

Lois and Ray—They were tourists...and in way over their heads.

Marta—She was always at the wrong place at the right time.

Han and Freya—They watched their child like a hawk.

Patty, Ellen, Linda and Stella—The four ladies from Indiana wanted the adventure of a lifetime...or did they?

Prologue

He began to climb the cliff, reaching from one handhold to the next with reckless abandon. Excitement made him disregard any possible danger. Pebbles dislodged by his hands and feet bounced away, disturbing other stones, which rattled down deep into the gorge below him.

His eyes, blurry with sweat and dust, almost missed the narrow opening. It looked impossible for anyone but a small child to pass through, but he was determined. He bloodied his stomach and back dragging himself into the slit in the rock.

Heedless of the pain, he looked around the small cave. It was hot, gloomy and almost without oxygen, but it *was* here, just as he'd known it would be. He bent nearly double to keep from banging his head on the jagged rock ceiling. The curtain of stone that obscured the entrance also cut off the bright desert sun. He switched on his flashlight, allowing his eyes a few precious moments to adjust.

The cave was shallow but riddled with narrow breaks in the rock face. He sucked in a deep breath of stale air and fell to his knees to consider. Then, methodically, he began to search every opening, forgetting about the snakes and scorpions, forgetting the cautions he'd had drummed into him since he'd arrived in Egypt.

The whole right-hand wall yielded no secrets.

What if it wasn't here? What if Ford was right, and he was risking his professional reputation, not to mention his life, for nothing?

But he *wasn't* wrong! He knew it, felt it, with every bone in his body.

The rock face scraped skin off his fingers as he groped blindly inside the next hole. Nothing. He sat back on his heels, dazed with disbelief. *He couldn't be wrong, damn it!*

He threw himself flat on the floor of the cave to wriggle both hands into the openings along the edge of the wall. Then, miraculously, the fingers of his left hand brushed something smooth, like metal and polished stone.

Paralyzed by excitement, he suddenly couldn't move. This was it! The discovery of a lifetime. The discovery that would establish him forever among the ranks of archaeology's greats: Carter, Belgoni, Harris.

His body shaking with tension, his shallow quick breathing echoing in his ears, he inched the object from its hiding place. Suddenly it was free, and he reverently balanced his treasure on his knees, staring at it with disbelief and wonder. The gold and jewels encrusting the box blazed in a dazzling display of colors and lights even after being hidden for thousands of years.

He *knew* this was it—the puzzle box wherein rested the hand of the ancient god Osiris. According to legend, Isis had fashioned a golden hand to complete the remains of her slain husband, Osiris. That hand had granted him eternal life.

For centuries, Egyptians had been captivated by the story of eternal love and its powers of renewal. Even now, there was a growing fanatical cult who believed that, by using authentic artifacts and the proper incantations, they, like Osiris, could be resurrected. It seemed crazy, but such was the power of the myth.

He himself had always been intrigued by the tale. But no myth led him here—it was hard work, years of research, listening to every story, every digger, following up the slightest clue, and finally depending on his intuition that had garnered results. Ford, the old skeptic, would be astonished! And Olivia would be so proud of him...

For a brief moment, he was so overwhelmed with emotion, he couldn't stop himself from shaking. Then a terrible realization came to him. He wasn't shaking at all.

The earth was shaking around him!

A crash deafened him. Rocks rumbled and the earth groaned beneath him. Then the walls of the cave began to move, crushing together. He felt the floor give way and he struggled to his feet, trying to escape. The ground opened and he fell, tumbling over and over, down into blackness.

Suddenly he felt one hand and then another and another. Hands reaching out to him, breaking his fall. Dozens of hands reaching out to take him.

Chapter One

Olivia Cranston sat up in bed, threw her arms over her head and screamed. She couldn't breathe, and her arms and shoulders ached from some great pressure weighing her down, threatening to destroy her. She had to hold it back, she had to survive!

Then, as suddenly as the terror had come, invading her dreamless sleep, pushing her into this waking nightmare, it fled.

Exhausted, she collapsed onto her pillows. Slowly the room came into focus. Her queen-size brass bed steadied beneath her. She could breathe again, in and out, in deep even breaths. The air was no longer dusty and stale, but scented with spicy exotic perfume—her signature scent, or so the staff at the Cranston Design Studio called it.

No longer was she huddled in a cramped black hole; but back in her bedroom with the geometric-patterned wallpaper and matching drapes she'd designed last season after her graduate work in Paris. The mirror in the antique french armoire reflected her pale face, her black hair, freed from its usual band, curling wildly and her amethyst eyes huge with fright. She looked around, searching for a grasp on reality. The digital clock on her bedside table glowed 7 a.m.

That meant it was midafternoon in Egypt. What had Charlie gotten himself into this time?

She rolled onto her side to grab the phone and punch in the number of the Archaeological Institute at the Cairo Museum of Antiquities, where her brother worked. After what seemed to be an interminable wait, the operator came on. Olivia cleared her throat of the lingering tightness. "Person to person to Dr. Charles Cranston, please."

The inevitable delays when calling the Middle East drove her crazy most days, but this morning she went wild. She got out of bed, and pacing the carpet as far as the phone cord would stretch, she cursed Egypt under her breath, cursed this link with her twin that had haunted them both from birth, cursed Charlie's insatiable curiosity.

"Please hold. I'm still trying to reach your party." The operator's voice, sounding tinny and far away, barely came through.

Resigned, Olivia threw herself on the bed, remembering all the other times she'd played this scene, waiting in fear for her brother's safety. Charlie was the elder by six minutes. Why didn't *he* get to live *her* pain? The connection had reversed itself only twice. The first time, Charlie had rushed to an emergency room doubled over in agony while she was having her appendix out four hundred miles away at her college hospital. The second time had been last summer when she'd fainted after stupidly dragging herself out of bed during a bout of twenty-four-hour flu to teach a drawing class at the inner-city youth center; Charlie had passed out in the Cairo museum, in midsentence as he was talking to his idol, Dr. Fordham I. Harris.

They had commiserated via telephone, hospital bed to hospital bed; she, in Chicago suffering from dehydration, and he, in Cairo suffering a mild concussion from banging his head on a display case as he collapsed.

Now what would they be commiserating about? Just what kind of trouble had he gotten himself into this time?

"I regret all lines to Egypt are down due to the earthquake."

Whatever else the operator continued to say became a blur of sound to Olivia. *Earthquake.* She sat up abruptly—that's what the terror had been! Charlie in an earthquake and she had felt the effects.

But there was something more. Something she didn't quite understand, but recognized—that little sting of fear smack in the middle of her stomach.

She replaced the phone and grabbed her remote. CNN already had the full story of the quake, which measured six point two on the Richter scale, that had rocked Egypt within the last hour. The screen showed rubble that had once been apartment houses in Cairo; thankfully, no public buildings were reported destroyed. That meant the museum where the Institute office was housed hadn't sustained any damage.

So, where was Charlie? Had he been in Cairo or was he out at a dig? Was he safe now?

She had no sense of her brother's presence. As they had aged, the intuitive bond they shared had stretched pretty thin, yet she always had a nagging awareness of Charlie. Now its absence frightened her.

Coming to one of her notoriously quick decisions, she left a message on voice mail for her office staff and called the airline to make travel arrangements. She could be in Cairo before the Egyptian phone lines were even repaired.

She kept the television on while she packed, bathed and dressed, trying to get more details on the quake. She even attempted another phone call but still couldn't get through.

In desperation, she lay down on her bed and tried to reach Charlie by concentrating, calling to him telepathically. Even though they'd given up this trick during adolescence because it never seemed to work, her desperation called for desperate measures. She'd picked up something this morning. Wow, had she! She shuddered, just remembering.

Maybe she could do it again. If she just had a sense that Charlie was okay, instead of this uncertain void, she could save herself a trip.

All she received for her trouble was a big fat nothing. Whatever the nature of their link, the connection had been severed.

Precisely at ten the doorman arrived to take her luggage to a waiting cab. "Good-mornin', Miss Cranston. I brought up your mail."

"Thanks, Marty. How's the arthritis today?" Eyeing him as he swung the heavy garment bag over his sloping shoulders, she decided to sit on her big suitcase; she'd pull it to the elevator herself before she'd let him hurt himself.

"I'm just fine, Miss Cranston." He laughed, low and husky, a smoker's growl. "Don't you want me to take that big one you're sittin' on?"

"No, just the garment bag and the small train case. I'll bring this one myself after I put a few more things in. I want to look through the mail before I leave."

Shaking his head, he mumbled under his breath as he stalked out. "Newfangled . . . independent . . ."

Those labels weren't new to Olivia and she wore them easily. With a brother like Charlie, she'd had to.

Cupping the pile of mail in her arms, she walked to her desk and dumped it on the neat surface. She turned to retrieve her bag, but stopped, looking at the mess. It pained her to leave her desk like this. After silently acknowledging that the obsessively organized behavior everyone accused her of was absolutely true, she turned back to quickly file her mail in its proper place. Junk mail in the round file, interesting catalogs in the magazine rack next to her desk chair, bills in the "in" box and personal letters in her drawer.

Right at the front was the thin stack of letters she'd received from her brother since he'd been in Egypt. She pulled them out and spread them on her bed. His sprawling, run-together sentences, interspersed with sketches and hieroglyphs that took forever to decipher, were somewhat reassuring. On impulse she decided to take them with her on the plane.

She lugged the big suitcase to the elevator and went down to meet the cab. But the letters burned a hole in her purse, so she took them out to study on the way to the airport. As always, Charlie's enthusiasm for archaeology and his obsession with his latest theory jumped off the pages. In the last letter, dated a month ago, Charlie implied he had had a falling-out with his idol, the brilliant Dr. Harris. Funny, she didn't remember noticing that the first time she'd read the letter.

She stuffed the envelopes back into her shoulder bag and closed her eyes. If she couldn't find Charlie when she arrived in Cairo, she would look up Dr. Fordham Harris. Surely he would know what her brother was up to.

Time became a blur for Olivia. First there was a flight from Chicago to Paris to endure, then a lengthy stopover before flying to Athens, and the interminable wait until the Cairo airport opened. She argued her way onto the first flight to Egypt and, afraid someone might try to displace her, she hovered around the gate, pacing restlessly for eight hours.

She hated flying. She felt punchy from jet lag and sheer exhaustion, yet she couldn't rest. Her fear for Charlie just wouldn't stop growing no matter how hard she tried to kill it with cold rationality.

But she didn't feel any better on arriving in Cairo. She still had no "sense" of Charlie. Absorbed in her worry, she didn't fully grasp what the passport official was trying to tell her.

"You must step out of line and follow the officer. Stand aside, please!" An interpreter appeared and waved her after a departing uniformed official.

Her luggage appeared out of nowhere and she followed the man, somewhat dazed, as everyone else from her flight had their passports routinely stamped and were on their way.

Olivia was taken to a side room where a bank of computers filled one wall. A swarthy man wearing a gray uniform stared down at her passport picture, up at her and back down again.

"Is there a problem?" She felt pleased that some remnant of her normal voice could squeeze through her tight, tense throat.

"Come with me!" he grunted. He turned on his heels, obviously expecting her to follow.

Only then did she notice another man, taller and broader, dressed in the same uniform, falling into step beside her. Hemmed in by them, she had no choice but to follow. They led her along one dingy corridor after another, down a flight of narrow stairs, through a long tunnel that seemed to go on forever, until they reached another staircase, which led to an unmarked wooden door.

"Wait here," the taller guard commanded, pushing the door open. Before he slammed it shut, she caught a glimpse of another computer. Somehow, that sign of civilization reassured her.

Maybe this was just some kind of formality. Maybe she'd neglected some visa requirement, or something, in her eagerness to get to her brother. Or maybe she was in deep trouble.

Suddenly remembering every horror story she'd ever heard about tourists alone in foreign countries, she took an involuntary step toward the closed door.

The remaining guard shifted his body, blocking her way.

"What's going on in there?" she demanded.

"Wait!" He pointed to a cracked black leather chair next to a low table covered with newspapers.

Resigned, Olivia slid down into the low chair. She placed her train case at her feet. The other two pieces of her luggage were set against the wall. She could tell by the man's remote eyes and rigid face that she wouldn't get anything out of him.

To control a new fear fluttering along her nerves, she sifted through the newspapers. French. Greek. Chinese. Russian. Impulsively she gathered them together and stacked them in one neat pile. Reaching down, she scooped up two folded sheets that had slipped under the table.

One was printed in English. The front page was devoted to earthquake stories. She devoured every word as the door remained ominously closed. Her jailer—she couldn't think of him as anything else—stared at her, his arms folded across his chest. Trying to ignore him, she flipped over the paper and continued to read.

Halfway down the page, a headline caught her eye. *Tablet from Book of the Dead Stolen from Museum of Antiquities.* The story from last week quoted Dr. Harris and mentioned her brother and his sudden absence from the Institute. She didn't like the sound of that at all! Was her brother a suspect—and was that why she was being detained?

Suddenly desperate, she surged to her feet and glared at her jailer with renewed spirit. "I demand to see someone in charge!"

His smile was insulting. A hot angry flush rose from her toes to the silver band restraining her hair. She'd busted the jaw of the first boy who had leered at her chest the way this man did. That incident, in the sixth grade, had earned her several afternoons of study hall and a stern lecture from her mother.

At last the door opened and the first officer stepped out. She thought she saw two others in that mysterious room but he shut the door too quickly for her to be certain.

"You may go now, Miss Cranston." He handed back her passport with a polite bow that was in sharp contrast to the other guard's rude stare.

She considered demanding to know why they had held her, but refrained. Instinctively she knew it had to do with her brother and the stolen artifact.

Each guard picked up a case and they escorted her to a door at the end of the hall. Suddenly she found herself out on the sidewalk at the perimeter of the airport. There wasn't a soul, much less a taxi, in sight.

She attached her shoulder straps to the suitcases and hefted them herself. After she'd walked the equivalent of six city blocks, she finally heard some life. Rounding a corner, she came to the main terminal building. Taking her life in her hands, she stepped off the curb, out into traffic, and tried to hail a cab the way she did every day in Chicago. From the shrieking brakes and horn blasts, she decided things were done differently here.

Resigned to finding a queue, she paraded the length of the terminal. At last a taxi stopped in front of her. The driver jumped out, courteously took her bags, stuffed them into his tiny trunk and motioned her to get in.

He said something unintelligible and she enunciated, "The Museum of Antiquities, please."

The streets of the city were packed with people and she was jarred by the strangeness of this place she'd so impulsively run off to. Everywhere she looked there were men: men sitting on the sidewalk smoking water pipes, men hunched over small tables in coffee-houses, men swaggering along the sidewalk. The few women she saw were covered from head to foot in black. Only their eyes were visible; dark and watchful eyes that made her very uncomfortable.

In fact, she had the feeling that everyone was watching her. She glanced over at the cars pressed close on either side and discovered both were filled with men who were all peering at her. She jerked her head round, refusing to look behind her. No doubt it was all her imagination, the seed planted by the bewildering treatment she'd received at the airport and the mention of her brother in the paper. Were men like those guards holding Charlie somewhere?

She told herself not to be paranoid and to take in the sights around her, even if she was in the middle of a nightmare traffic jam. At one point, they had to stop for five minutes in the middle of an intersection. Mercedes sedans flitted in and out between donkey carts, buses and horse-drawn carriages. One cart driver forced a poor animal in front of a tour bus, where there seemed to be no room, so he could make a U-turn to get back practically to the same spot in the congested traffic.

A white-robed man sauntered past, balancing a flat board piled impossibly high with round loaves of bread. She found their symmetry, which defied gravity and motion, fascinating.

Shaking his head and muttering under his breath, the cabdriver finally pulled to a stop. "Museum. You go."

She jumped out on the busy street, anxious to get to the museum.

Frightened by the stares of men pressing around her on the sidewalk, Olivia breathed a deep sigh of relief when she finally reached her destination. The woman behind the information desk took one look at all the luggage Olivia hauled in with her and shook her head.

"I'm sorry. You can't take those into the museum."

Between fear for Charlie and the horrible irrational feeling that everyone in Cairo was out to get her, Olivia felt ready to collapse. She sagged against the highly polished wooden counter.

"I'm Olivia Cranston. My brother is Dr. Charles Cranston. Could you direct me to the Institute offices here?"

At last someone in this godforsaken country smiled at her. "I'm afraid your brother is away. But you can find his superior, Dr. Fordham Harris, in the jewel room. I'll keep your luggage here for you."

Olivia followed the woman's directions through a maze of hallways. For the first time in almost two days, she began to feel a little optimistic. Surely Dr. Harris would know where she could find Charlie. Unless... how serious, she wondered, had his falling-out with her brother been? She also questioned whether it had something to do with that newspaper article.

The jewel room held only one person. She caught her breath in surprise. *This* was the illustrious Dr. Harris? No male model of her acquaintance, not even the bodybuilders at her health club, had this man's combination of height, broad shoulders and slim waist. His curly blond hair hugged a bronzed face with sculpted features dominated by bright blue eyes.

He had a case open and slipped something into his trouser pocket. Just as she stepped through the doors, she saw a flash of carnelian and gold. A necklace?

But in her anxiety about Charlie, she dismissed what she had seen as unimportant. At last here was someone who could help her.

HEARING FOOTSTEPS, Ford spun around, the amulet heavy against his thigh. A vision navigated her way toward him through the I Dynasty display cases of jewelry, making the precious stuff seem pale in comparison.

His eyes roved over her long, lithe body; the swirl of dark hair around the determined face; her glowing amethyst eyes. This female captivated him in the same powerful way the luminous Nefertiti had when he'd first seen her likeness, and run his caressing hands over her carved head.

However, this woman was flesh and blood. And, as odd as it seemed, he wanted her. Even in the middle of this mess. He labeled it love at first sight, or maybe it was lust at first glimpse.

"Dr. Harris, I'm Olivia Cranston."

He took her offered hand, gripping it with tight fingers, to reassure himself he wasn't in the middle of a dream.

Charlie always said he never carried a picture of his twin sister because it would be too narcissistic, like looking at himself. Poor young fool was deluding himself! While his hair was merely dark brown, Olivia's was a rich ebony and hung like a sable stole around her shoulders. Charlie's eyes were blue, his sister's an almost incandescent purple. The perfect oval of her face was masculinized in her brother by fuller cheeks. This woman should be compared only to the supreme goddess, Isis.

"Dr. Harris, are you all right?"

Apart from the fact that he'd stood staring at her for an unconscionable time, crushing her fingers while trying to decide how best to get her the hell out of Egypt before her presence complicated everything, Ford had never felt better.

He blurted out the first logical thought to come to him. "Olivia, how did you get here? The airport opened again only a few hours ago!"

She pulled her hand free and flung her head up in a regal pose worthy of a queen.

"I was waiting at the Athens airport for the first flight in. Where's my brother?"

A strange voice invaded their conversation. "A very good question. I have missed seeing the brilliant young Dr. Cranston the last few days."

Where the hell had Akim come from? Ford fumed. Had the man seen him take the amulet? Had Olivia?

Ford felt as guilty as an actual thief—which, he realized with chagrin, he now was, though only out of necessity. But perhaps that made him no better than a thief...no better than Charlie, if the young fool had actually stolen the priceless tablet from the Book of the Dead. Had he? Ford, not to mention Interpol, was beginning to suspect it was a possibility.

A knot of dread formed deep in Ford's gut. He could only hope Charlie hadn't become mixed up with those crazy cult people by choice. It seemed impossible, and yet Charlie was obsessed in trying to find the hand of Osiris, risking his reputation as a legitimate scientist as well as their friendship in his almost fanatical search for the artifact.

For all Ford knew, Charlie himself might have been the alleged cult member who had called him with the ransom deal. After all, holding a scientist hostage seemed bizarre at best. Was Charlie's life truly at stake? Or was he using Ford to secure the thet amulet?

"Miss Cranston, I congratulate you on your resourcefulness in arriving in my country at such a time." Akim, seemingly puzzled by Ford's distraction, took over, bowing deeply from the waist. A small smile flickered beneath his thick dark mustache. "Permit me to introduce myself, since Dr. Harris does not. I am Akim Tamaran, the second under secretary of the Antiquities Ministry."

"Then I feel sure you can help me."

The pure cool tone of her voice held fatigue and fear. Ford thought fast. "Akim doesn't keep track of the Institute staff. I do. Charlie isn't in Cairo at the moment." It was not exactly a lie. At least she turned those magnificent eyes back to him, though her fixed stare and lifted right eyebrow demanded more.

"He's gone upriver. Around Luxor. He's on holiday until next month's dig. I can't reach him because all the phone lines are down."

"Then I shall simply have to go find him myself." Her lush red mouth smiled with a sudden cold composure. "Good day, gentlemen."

She twirled away abruptly. Ford reached out to stop her and had his hand firmly rebuffed.

"Miss Cranston, please think but a moment," Akim offered in his soft voice of diplomatic reason.

Her hair whipped across her cheek as she turned back to face them. Ford dropped his outstretched hand and rammed it into his pocket. His fingers gripped the carved stone necklace...the necklace that just might save her brother's life.

"Akim means you can't just take off, traveling around Egypt alone at a time like this. It's not particularly safe for a western woman like you, even at the best of times. And this isn't one of those."

He almost laughed at the ridiculous understatement. He was having a hard enough time trying to figure out how to find Charlie without a beautiful woman tagging along. Olivia obviously feared for her brother's safety, yet she couldn't possibly guess the extent of the danger for everyone involved, especially if the wrong people discovered who she was.

His gaze deliberately starting at her flat black shoes, traveling up the slim legs that went on forever, to the narrow hips, and lingering on the beautiful breasts pushing against the fine knit of her sweater, Ford finally met her eyes. They were as determined as ever. The fact that she didn't pull her black-and-white jacket over her chest, embarrassed by his visual perusal, the way most women would have, made his thighs tighten.

A pure sensual heat sparked between them as they gazed at each other. The only other times in his life he could remember feeling the emotions in the air around him was at a dig when he uncovered a treasure buried for thousands of years. Unfortunately, he decided, Olivia was a treasure of a different sort. A treasure, but not for him. Not at this time and place.

"Then what do you suggest, Dr. Harris?" she purred, but her eyes pinned him with a loathing glare.

"I'm going to Luxor tomorrow." At least he could tell her that much of the truth. "I'll find Charlie and have him contact you in Cairo as soon as possible. Where are you staying?"

"The Mena House." She glanced from him to Akim's narrow aristocratic face and back again. "Is there any way I can accompany you to Luxor, Dr. Harris?"

He had to stall her until he could get out of the city. Not liking himself much, he nodded. "I'll see what I can do and notify you first thing in the morning."

Her eyes might be glassy from exhaustion but he saw them harden as she considered his answer. At last she gave him a ghost of a smile. Until then, he hadn't realized he'd been holding his breath.

"Fine. I'll expect to hear from you by morning."

He and Akim stood staring after her like two statues. Her body seemed to float across the floor, the soft sway of her hips mesmerizing.

"You know this magnificent woman well, my friend?" The polite inquiry came as close to avid curiosity about Ford's personal life as Akim would come. Such a slip in manners deserved an honest reply.

"I just met her. But I already wish she'd be the mother of my children."

Akim's eyelids snapped shut. Silently cursing his own stupidity, Ford reached out and clasped the man's shoulder. "I'm sorry, old friend. I know you still mourn the death of your wife and child."

"It is the will of the gods. I have been telling myself for eighteen months. Time will make all things right. Now it is your time to deal with Miss Cranston.

She doesn't appear to know anything about Charlie's misfortune."

Ford crushed the amulet between his fingers, feeling it heat up against his skin. "What are you talking about, Akim?"

His dark eyes were wide with sorrow as he spread his hands in a gesture of supplication. "Ford, my friend, everyone at the ministry knows Interpol is interested in questioning Charlie about this terrible theft."

"Interpol questioned the entire staff." Feeling on safer ground, Ford forced a smile. "Including me."

"Of course. You are right. Have a safe journey to Luxor, my friend," Akim said quietly before turning away.

Ford watched him go with a mixture of worry and suspicion. Did he know anything? Had he seen him take the amulet? he wondered again.

Deciding that the straitlaced Akim would turn him in if he suspected anything, despite their friendship, Ford made his escape. He had an appointment to keep. According to his instructions, he had to contact a certain Mr. Gameel Mujod about booking passage on the Emerald Empress sailing from Luxor to Aswân. He had no intention of calling Olivia at the Mena House.

After all, this journey might very well be only one way. For both him and Charlie.

Chapter Two

From her window in the Mena House, Olivia watched the rising sun touch first one, then another, then the last of the three great pyramids on the Giza plain. Looming over the historic hotel encircled by its stone walls, they were a constant reminder of the glory of ancient times. Somehow, she had imagined they would be lit, like an attraction at Disneyland. Instead, the eroding granite facades disappeared into the night, coming alive only at the kiss of the sun-god, Ra.

Sheer willpower, or perhaps it was stubbornness, kept her going this morning. She'd dozed on and off all the long night, waiting for Dr. Harris to call. At 6 a.m. she phoned the hotel operator, asking for messages. There were none. The fear she'd experienced waking up to Charlie's nightmare two—or was it three?—days ago was beginning to return.

At seven she ordered a large pot of coffee from room service. She could use the caffeine boost. Like so many young Egyptian men, the boy who brought her tray was darkly handsome with an infectious grin that widened when she handed him a generous baksheesh. She remembered reading in her guidebook that tourists in Egypt had to rely heavily on providing tips, or bribes.

The coffee smelled strong and looked like mud. There was no milk to dilute it, so she added two spoons of sugar. After one sip, she put the cup aside and picked up the English newspaper the hotel had provided. The headline was very reassuring—apparently the damage from the quake was slight. She scanned the page, then opened to the inside.

A picture in the right bottom corner of the page caught her eye. She stared at it in disbelief, rereading the caption beneath it to make sure she understood. *Thet Amulet Stolen Yesterday.*

Olivia sucked in her breath in sudden recognition. Carnelian and gold. The lovely antique necklace was the object she'd seen Dr. Harris push into his pants pocket yesterday when she'd arrived at the museum. Though she'd gotten only a glimpse, her designer's eye would never forget the shape and texture of such a priceless object. Now it was reported stolen!

She studied the picture closely, trying to convince herself she was mistaken. But she wasn't. Her artistic eye wouldn't let her deceive herself, even if the newspaper photo paled in comparison to the original.

Quickly she read the accompanying article. This was the second theft of a precious Egyptian artifact in less than a month. There were no leads in either incident.

Her mind raced with possibilities. Could there be a misunderstanding? Had Dr. Harris taken it for study, and not bothered to tell anyone? Highly unlikely.

Shaking, she stared at the picture until it became a blur. She had to make executive decisions every day. Why was she sitting here wasting time?

She tried the Institute office at the museum, calling every few minutes until finally, at eight, a woman answered. "Dr. Harris will be in Luxor until further notice."

Her words brought a hot flush of anger and fear roaring through Olivia's blood. Her hands trembled. That man had lied to her! He'd never had any intention of calling her. Slowly she replaced the receiver on its cradle. Perhaps she was the only person who knew that the renowned archaeologist, Dr. Fordham I. Harris, was nothing more than a common thief.

Suddenly a thought occurred to her that made her quake with even more anger. Perhaps because of his falling-out with Charlie, Dr. Harris had stolen the amulet to set up her brother. And to think, she had caught him in the act! He might be the one who had stolen the tablet from the Book of the Dead mentioned in the newspaper article.

His awkward silence upon first meeting her made sense now. Guilt. No wonder he was trying to get rid of her! They were the two people in all of Egypt who knew Charlie was incapable of stealing the artifacts that were his life's work—and who also knew that Dr. Harris was more than capable of such a theft!

The question now was, what should she do about it?

Her mind raced as she considered her options. She'd come to Egypt to find Charlie. Dr. Harris was her strongest and only lead to Charlie's whereabouts. He might be a thief and a liar, but remembering her treatment at the hands of the airport police, she decided she'd much prefer to take her chances with him than the local authorities.

Coming to the only decision that made any sense to her, she called the airport to book a flight to Luxor, dressed and checked out of the hotel in record time. In the taxi, she couldn't help glancing behind her. Nothing had changed since yesterday; she would swear that everywhere, dark eyes were watching her.

But this time, perhaps because she wasn't going through customs, the airport official barely spared her a glance before waving her forward. She ran to find the right gate for her flight, taking a ragged breath of relief, clutching her train case tightly. Through a window, an impossibly small unmarked silver plane shook violently as the pilots tested the engines. Surely this couldn't be her flight!

Shivers began, deep at her core. This airline was nothing like American or United. Would this plane even be able to take off or would it shake apart as it taxied down the runway?

She had to get to Luxor. She had to find Dr. Harris. He might lead her to Charlie. Whatever was going on, she had a sinking feeling her twin was smack-dab in the middle of it. He'd always had a knack for getting into trouble, ever since they were kids. Why should now be any different?

She steeled herself for the ordeal ahead, walked across the already baking tarmac and up the makeshift stairs. Myriad pairs of scowling dark eyes looked up as she entered the plane. The aircraft was packed. There were no assigned seats, so she scouted for a row where she might sit alone, not surrounded by disapproving men.

Toward the back of the plane, there appeared to be an empty space, but as she approached, she could see a man's long leg, covered in denim, extending into the aisle. A leg that seemed somehow familiar.

"Hello. Again," she said in a cool voice that covered her fury well.

Dr. Fordham Harris surged to his feet, his face hardening into a granite mask. "What in the hell are you doing here?"

"Looking for you." Realizing she was blocking the aisle to study him as though he were a fabric sample, she tore her eyes away and glanced around the airplane.

"Please be seated. We must prepare for takeoff now." The stewardess's directive forced him to allow Olivia to squeeze past to the window seat. She tried to do her best not to touch him, but the seats were closer than normal and her hip brushed against his. It felt as though a jolt of electricity jumped between them.

Ignoring that, she stored her train case securely under the seat in front of her, fastened her seat belt low and tight across her abdomen and... There wasn't a card with safety rules to study in the seat pocket in front of her! She took a deep breath, reminding herself not to panic.

Even with her mind wildly trying to figure out what was going on here with Charlie and Dr. Harris, her hatred of flying became as all-consuming as ever. She *really* hated flying. Always had, always would. She made herself do it—not only for business, but because she considered her fear a silly weakness that she could control.

"Don't worry." Although he still glared at her, he had enough decency to realize she was terrified. "I've flown this airline upriver for years. You're in good hands."

The reassurance was calculated to soften her attitude toward him. It didn't. Lifting her chin, she said curtly, "Listen, Dr. Harris—"

"Call me Ford. Charlie does. And for the last two years, I've called you Olivia."

His charm washed over her like a soft desert breeze. A tiny light danced suddenly in his eyes and Olivia became painfully conscious that mere inches separated them. He switched from anger to charm as easily as he'd slipped that stolen amulet into his pocket.

It would be wise to keep that memory in mind. Dr. Harris could be as charming as he wanted, but she knew who and what he was. She knew she couldn't trust him. The trick now would be to make herself immune to his charm... and the crackling sensual attraction she felt whenever they were together.

She leaned away as far as her seat allowed and met his eyes with her most accusing glare. "Ford, then. Let's lay our cards on the table. I'm here because I think my brother is in some kind of trouble. You obviously think so, too, or you wouldn't be going to Luxor to look for him."

He burst into a shout of laughter. "Me? Look for Charlie? He knows Egypt as well as I do. I told you, he's on holiday until the Institute dig starts up in the middle of next month. Trust me, we'll find him hanging around Luxor or the Valley of the Kings, talking archaeology with anyone who will listen."

His transparent denial infuriated her. She turned her face to the window, pretending to watch a huge 747 move out onto the taxiway so he couldn't see her anger. Trust him!

"I'm going to Luxor to do some preliminary work at Institute House," he said.

She stiffened, studying his reflection in the plane's window. Temper flared from his blue eyes. Good. He was obviously not pleased that she had followed him, though the tone of his next words belied his irritation.

"I'm also going to check for earthquake damage at Karnak," he went on in a light, charming voice, as if they were on the best of terms.

"I'm relieved to hear that, Ford." Until she discovered what game Ford was playing and what it might have to do with Charlie, she would have to let her instinct guide her. And her instinct now told her not to let him know she was on to him.

"Good. I'm glad that's settled." His smile broadened, but never reached his cool and watchful eyes. "Sorry I snapped at you. And sorry I didn't call you at the hotel. Last night I realized Charlie wouldn't want you to be roaming around Egypt on your own right now. I'll make contact with him and then he'll join you in Cairo. You can take the morning flight back tomorrow."

"I think I'll spend a few days in Luxor first." Widening her eyes, she hoped she looked only innocently curious. "Where do you suggest I stay for a few days? Who knows, by then Charlie might show up."

"Yeah, who knows." The chill in his voice made her pulse accelerate. He looked directly at her, his eyes very blue in his tanned face, his mouth almost cruel. "If you're determined to stay despite my warnings, I suggest the Winter Palace. It was the mecca of leisure travel in Egypt during the colonial period, a favorite haunt of Agatha Christie, the mystery novelist."

"That sounds lovely."

She put her head back and closed her eyes, clenching her fists momentarily as the plane revved up for takeoff. The pulsing engines resounded through her; the little plane vibrated as if it might shake itself apart. She kept her eyes closed, trying to visualize a nice, easy train ride. Even after the plane leveled off, she kept her eyes closed so she wouldn't have to deal with Ford.

Mercifully, he didn't try to engage her in conversation. She felt him study her from time to time, but perversely refused to look at him. She didn't want to give away her complete distrust of him.

Suddenly the vague awareness of Charlie returned. That was some comfort. She hadn't realized how tense she'd been until she relaxed behind the blackness of her eyelids. At least she knew Charlie was alive.

In a moment she fell sound asleep.

"Olivia, we're in Luxor."

She was awakened by Ford's voice, low and soft in her ear, his breath fanning her cheek. During the flight, she had unconsciously shifted to use Ford's broad, strong shoulder as a pillow. She could smell his cologne, a light limy scent that reminded her of fresh tropical air. His face had softened and his mouth curled in a smile. Charm again.

"C'mon, Olivia. We've got to get off now."

Jet lag made her feel almost drugged as she followed Ford's lead; she even allowed him to carry her case. He traveled light, using one hand to sling his black leather tote over one shoulder and guiding her with the other hand through the inevitable airport formalities. Even though these were simpler here than in Cairo, she couldn't shake the uneasy feeling that she was being watched. She glanced around, expecting trouble.

"What's wrong?" he asked, once they were standing in front of the small terminal. The hot sun felt oppressive, even in the shade of the overhanging roof. People kept jostling her, making it hard to hang on to her composure.

"Nothing." She sighed, darting quick looks at the people milling around her, shouting in languages she didn't understand. "What should I do now?"

He glanced down at his watch and back to her with a reluctant glare. "Okay. I'll drop you at the Winter Palace." His arm shot out and a cab shrieked to a halt in front of them.

"Where are *you* going?" She threw the question over her shoulder as he pushed her into the back seat.

"I told you, I have Institute business."

Suddenly he was clipped and curt again. This shifting back and forth was too much! She tried to ask some harmless questions about Luxor but, except for some unintelligible conversation with the driver, he had clammed up.

Resigned to his silent treatment for the moment, she stared out the window. From the plane, Luxor had appeared to be a strip of verdant green in the middle of a golden desert, with the Nile River weaving serenely through it. But as she traveled its streets, she could see it was a bustling place. Hotels faced the east bank, set back from the river by a wide corniche, like any other tourist town.

She sat forward and pressed her face to the dusty window. There was a crowded bazaar, its sounds and colors enticing. Women, again robed in black, balancing baskets of provisions from the market on their heads, moved along the side of the road. There were as many horses and carriages in the streets as automobiles.

The cab halted in front of a dusty white building with a semicircle of small shops guarding its entrance. The hotel seemed a bit down-at-heel. Even the lobby was unimpressive. But through double doors, she could look down onto a well-watered garden of remarkable design and beauty.

A wizened old man who turned out to be the busboy rushed over as Ford dumped Olivia's luggage at her feet.

"Stay here. I'll be in touch when I can," he commanded and turned, left the lobby and jumped into the waiting cab.

Furious at the way he felt he could simply dismiss her, she thrust some Egyptian currency into the old man's lined palm. "Watch my luggage, please. I'll be back."

A queue of cabs waited outside and she jumped into the first one. Feeling slightly foolish, she leaned forward, hoping the driver spoke English. "Follow that blue cab!"

She thrust some bills in front of his nose, which vanished instantly. They roared out into traffic in pursuit, careening around corners, taking her away from the Nile and into a part of the city that seemed dark and frightening.

FORD ROLLED his shoulders, taking long, deep breaths of the taxi's air, smoky from the driver's strong cigarettes. How had he gotten into this mess? And how was he going to keep Olivia out of it? After this morning he didn't, couldn't, trust her to stay put. Maybe once he'd taken this step, he'd have a better idea what he had to do next.

The Mujod Tours office was in one of the modern, ugly buildings on the upper corniche. He walked into the lobby, checking for an alternate exit, surreptitiously looking for a tail. He fingered the amulet in his pocket. Would the switch be made now? Could it be that simple?

He really wasn't prepared for this at all. No weapon, no backup...where the hell was Interpol? He marched into the office.

A slender young woman looked up from her desk. "Good day. May I help you?" Her wide smile flashed beautiful, even, white teeth.

"My name's Fordham Harris. I need to talk to Gameel Mujod about booking passage on the Emerald Empress."

She recoiled from the harsh edge in his voice.

Ford decided there wasn't an ounce of subtlety in him and tried to soften his tone. He had to find a way to follow the instructions the caller had given him. Smiling through gritted teeth, he asked, "Is Mr. Mujod in?"

"Yes. Just a moment, please."

She disappeared through a wood-paneled door. Ford looked around, studying the layout as he might a dig site. He searched for the unexpected, anything that didn't fit that could give him a clue where to find what he searched for.

The trouble was, he didn't know what to expect; all this cloak-and-dagger stuff was new to him.

The business appeared to be exactly what it claimed—a prosperous tour office with framed travel posters covering the walls and brochures stacked on the tables next to overstuffed chairs. He stiffened when the door swung open, then unwound abruptly. The short squat man with thick graying hair who stepped forward couldn't possibly have anything to do with a strange cult that believed in resurrection!

Could he? Ford couldn't quite read the expression on Mujod's full face—was the man surprised to see him or was he a part of this whole deal? Perhaps he was even the Interpol contact that agency had promised would get in touch with him.

"Dr. Harris, it is indeed you." When Mujod bowed, Ford saw the top of his bald head. "This is a great honor. Please, come into my private office and be seated."

Settled in a carved chair with pillows tucked behind his back and a strong cup of tea at his side, Ford swept his eyes around the room. The rich carpet, the elaborate brass tea service on an inlaid table, even the young woman out front all indicated the tour business had made Mr. Mujod a wealthy man.

Mujod sat behind his wide desk. "How may I serve you?"

"I want to sail on the Emerald Empress tomorrow."

"A fine choice, Dr. Harris. The Emerald Empress is the jewel of the S&B fleet. The ship will embark for

Dendera tomorrow morning, then come back to Luxor to visit Karnak before heading upriver to Edfu. When she reaches Aswân, we will tour Philae, the dam and..." He chuckled deep in his chest. "Pardon me, Dr. Harris, of course *you* know all the delights that await visitors in Aswân."

The guy was good, Ford had to give him that. Nothing in his placid face or ingratiating voice told whether he might be a player in the game.

"I cannot believe this tour will offer you any insight into Egypt, Dr. Harris."

Ford shrugged. "Call it a busman's holiday."

Mujod glanced at him, apparently puzzled.

"Sorry, it's an American term." Ford leaned forward and placed the delicate teacup on the edge of the desk. "I need a break and I want to take this trip tomorrow. Is there room?"

"Of course. We will make room for such a distinguished guest," Mujod declared, surging to his feet. "Perhaps you would honor us by giving a brief lecture or two about some of the sites we shall visit."

He hated being manipulated, yet how could he refuse? Meeting Mujod's squinty eyes, Ford nodded slowly. "Sure. We archaeologists just love to talk shop."

"You do us too much honor." Mujod bowed all the way to the door, making Ford uneasy. "Please excuse me, Dr. Harris. I will personally get the necessary papers from the outer office."

He jumped to his feet, then sat back abruptly, disappointed that this was apparently not where arrangements for the switch were to be made. This whole setup reeked. The sooner he got out of here, the sooner he could take some action. To hell with Interpol, and to hell with the damn cult.

He would do what he should have done at the beginning. Find Charlie himself.

OLIVIA GLANCED UP from the Nile-tour brochures she was pretending to leaf through when a man rushed into the outer office.

"An honor." He rubbed his hands together with glee. "That such an esteemed archaeologist as Dr. Harris should take our tour on the Emerald Empress! I fear I shall be nervous to guide him. He is so much more knowledgeable than I."

The young woman looked astounded that her boss should be so flustered.

"Quickly, Farita," the man snapped, "give me the necessary forms for the cruise and for the Winter Palace. We will put him in the best room, the presidential suite overlooking the gardens and the Nile!"

The strange little man didn't spare Olivia a glance as he twirled away, sheets of paper clutched in his pudgy hand, and disappeared again behind the impressive wooden door.

The woman, Farita, looked up at Olivia with wide dark eyes. "I apologize for any delay. May I help you decide, now that you've had a chance to look over our brochures?"

Olivia had followed Ford here with no particular plan in mind. She just wanted to know where he was off to in such a hurry. Now she stared blankly at Farita, speculating wildly. Why would a man who knew Egypt like the back of his hand go on a Nile cruise?

Especially when he was supposed to be on Institute business?

It didn't make sense—yet neither had anything else she'd seen or heard him do. Which meant she had to stay with him until she could fit all the pieces together. The theft, her brother, the cruise...somewhere they were bound to connect.

"I'd like to book passage on the Emerald Empress."

Farita's sweet laughter made Olivia smile despite the tension clawing at her stomach. "You are the second passenger to book today. You are fortunate there is a place left on this cruise. It is one of our finest and leaves tomorrow. Please, there are many forms that must be filled out."

Olivia hurried, not wishing to be caught by Ford until it was too late for him to stop her.

"Very good, Miss Cranston." The young woman nodded, looking over the sheets of paper. "Now all I must do is make a reservation for you at the Winter Palace."

"I'll make it myself. They are already holding my luggage." She knew exactly what room she wanted. "When will the tour begin?"

"This afternoon at two, all passengers booked on the tour will meet for orientation in the private parlor at the Winter Palace. I look forward to seeing you then, Miss Cranston."

Olivia slipped out the door and glanced at her watch. That gave her an hour to carry out her own plan.

Chapter Three

It took her thirty minutes of cajoling and a baksheesh that she felt sure would keep the desk clerk smiling for weeks, before he'd give her the room next to Dr. Harris. But she prevailed!

Her room faced the Nile and the view was truly breathtaking. She was on the curve of the building, able to see both the surprisingly lush gardens and the Nile. The suite next door spanned the entire width of the hotel, cutting off the other side completely. Dr. Harris must be as important and famous as Charlie had said.

Why would a man with such a reputation have stolen from the museum? After all, he had everything to lose if caught. None of this made any sense to her.

She stared out her window. Feluccas glided on the water, their sails mute testimony to a time long ago. Across the river, the green of the fertile Nile valley stopped abruptly as if it had hit an invisible and impregnable barrier. Beyond rose the rock wall that concealed the desert and famed necropolis, the Valley of the Kings.

All seemed peaceful in the hot afternoon sun. The exotic sights and sounds were more fascinating than she'd imagined, even after listening to her brother rave about Egypt. Maybe if this were a normal tourist visit, she could begin to understand some of Charlie's fascination for the place. But nothing about this visit could be called normal.

Quickly she splashed water on her face and pulled a comb through her hair before making her way downstairs.

"Miss Cranston?" Farita greeted her at the double doors to a small paneled sitting room. "Please join us."

With an ease born of dealing with buyers, manufacturers, suppliers, artists and her own staff, Olivia entered the room full of strangers. She found herself sympathizing with the young guide's task. No one in the circle of eleven people was smiling, including the guide. A glance around told her Ford was not among the group.

"Please, if you need anything or have any questions, just ask for me," Farita announced. "I shall be your leader for our journey along the Nile. Everyone in our group is English-speaking. I would like each of you to introduce yourself and tell where you are from."

An expensively dressed older couple introduced themselves as Lois and Ray from Naples, Florida. A slightly younger, but more sober man and woman introduced themselves as Freya and Han from South Africa, and the blond woman beside them as their daughter, Marta.

A sour-faced young man sprawling in his chair appeared to be paying no attention. Yet he squinted and glanced slowly around the group when his turn came. "I am Stephen Phipps from Manchester, England." Beside him, the squat woman in sensible shoes, a khaki split skirt, crisp white blouse, holding a pith helmet on her lap, was his Aunt Irmentrude.

Then came four women from Indiana: Linda, Stella and Ellen, traveling with her mother-in-law, Patty, who looked as though she could run circles around the younger women.

Finally, it was her turn. "I'm Olivia Cranston from Chicago."

Lois gasped. "I have one of your pillows! You know, Ray, the one with all the bright colors and the funny squiggly designs on it."

Everyone in the room turned their attention to her. "I'm a designer," she explained, favoring them all with a tight smile. "I'm glad you're enjoying the pillow, Lois."

"This is very good." Farita nodded. "Already we know one another. For what is left of this afternoon, we will take a stroll through the bazaar to the Luxor Museum."

Where could Ford be? Frantic to find out, Olivia stood in the center of the room as the others, like the schoolchildren she'd seen in Cairo, filed out obediently.

Farita waited at the door. "Miss Cranston?"

"Where's Dr. Harris? I thought he was on this tour!" she blurted out before she could stop herself. She hadn't wanted to be so obvious.

"Dr. Harris will be joining us later. Please come now, Miss Cranston."

Olivia joined the rest of the tour but found herself lagging behind, looking for someone who might be following her, looking for someone who might be trying to catch up with the tour, looking for *him*.

She told herself to be patient. Taking long deep breaths, she shut off her mind and looked around in earnest to get her bearings. Unlike modern Cairo, Luxor was the stuff of exotic and mysterious dreams of faraway places. The group tracked through narrow streets that twisted this way and that under the shadow of stone arches. In the bazaar, merchandise spilled out of tented stalls; hawkers touted galabeas, the long hooded garments sported by natives—some colorful and cheap-looking, others elaborately embroidered by hand, and still others, beautiful, filmy and shot with gold thread. There were vendors with brass pots, inlaid wooden boxes and even artifacts from tombs, which everyone, buyers and sellers alike, knew were fake.

Olivia stopped to examine some carved scarabs for their sheer beauty. A vision of a silk scarf with such a design in lapis and sand leaped into her mind. She pulled out a notebook from her shoulder bag and began sketching.

She had filled two sheets when someone bumped against her. She glanced up and found herself surrounded. Men with dark eyes pressed in on her. She caught her breath in surprise and then fear, remembering how in Cairo she'd felt as if people watched and followed her. Now that feeling returned tenfold. She stepped forward, trying to break through the circle, but the men moved with her. The heat, the odor of the bodies pressing in on her, made her pulse pound in her throat. She felt light-headed as she twisted one way and then another trying to find an opening in the crowd.

Suddenly she heard her name called. Farita pushed her way through the circle of hawkers. "Come along, Miss Cranston. You really must try to stay with the group."

Olivia was startled to realize there really had been no threat, just an overeager group of merchants that had discovered an inexperienced tourist who had been left behind. Up the street, the rest of her tour waited for her.

"Sorry," she gasped, the hot dry air rasping in her throat.

Although Farita smiled at her, she noticed some of the others did not. Feeling chastised, she kept pace for a while. But then she fell behind again as she searched each side street for a sign of Ford, or anything to give her some clue what she should do next.

"Miss Cranston? Is there a problem?" Farita took Olivia's arm and urged her forward.

"You needn't be worried if I don't stay with the group. I can find my way back to the hotel just fine."

The guide shook her head. "I am sure you are capable of finding your way. But, please, for these few days, let me advise you."

Farita's sweet concern forced Olivia to nod in agreement.

A block before they reached the museum, Olivia glanced down a side street and saw a small wooden sign for Institute House, Charlie's home away from home. He had spent months here. Surely she would get some sense of his whereabouts if she could find a way to check the place out. Besides, Ford might be there!

Already plotting, she paid only desultory attention when they reached the museum, until she came upon the Talatat's wall. The two-hundred-and-eighty-three-block limestone relief showing Akhenaton and Nefertiti worshipping Aton was most unusual for its scenes of everyday palace life. The likenesses of the royal couple in particular caught her attention. Less formalized than much of Egyptian art, these two figures seemed to come alive for her for some reason.

Olivia stood at the wall and began sketching. The tour moved farther and farther off. After a few moments, they were out of sight.

She moved quickly back the way she had entered, intent on leaving before anyone saw her.

She sidestepped a statue and squeezed out the entrance gate. Only Marta and Stephen, who also were paying no attention to Farita's running lecture, sending each other furtive glances, instead, might have noticed her slip out of the museum. She felt guilty about Farita, and decided to return to the hotel before dark so the young guide wouldn't worry too much. By then, she hoped she would have picked up Ford's trail.

Retracing her steps, she found the side street with no problem. Institute House sat behind a high brick wall with an iron gate. Fortunately, the gate stood slightly ajar, so she entered. Inside the building, her shoes clattered on the granite floor, announcing her arrival.

A secretary looked up from an enormous pile of papers and greeted her with a polite smile.

"May I help you?" A cool voice matched the woman's austere face.

"Yes. I'm Olivia Cranston. I'm looking for my brother, Dr. Charles Cranston."

"My, my. I can see the resemblance. I'm sorry, Miss Cranston, didn't he know you were coming? Your brother has been out of Luxor on holiday for the past fortnight. For any further information, you will need to speak with Dr. Harris, the head of the Institute. You are very fortunate that he is in town at present."

Olivia tried to hide her excitement. He was still here! "Could I see Dr. Harris now?"

"Presently he is out of the office." The words sounded rehearsed.

Olivia smiled as a scheme occurred to her. "Could I wait for him in his office?" All she needed was a few moments to look around.

The secretary sniffed and squared her thin shoulders beneath a high-necked, starched white blouse. "That is quite impossible. Would you care to make an appointment?"

Olivia wasn't about to give up so easily. Leaning forward, she pressed on. "Ford assured me Charlie is only away on holiday. But perhaps you might know something more that—"

"Miss Cranston, I'm surprised at you." The pinched-faced woman pushed her wire-rimmed glasses to the tip of her sharp nose and gave Olivia a look that could roast a marshmallow. "As I said already, if you wish to speak with Dr. Harris about your concerns, I would be happy to arrange an appointment for you."

Deciding to cut her losses, she smiled politely. "No, thank you. I appreciate your time." She backed out the door and looked around for a police station.

On her own, she was getting nowhere fast. She needed help. Surely there *had* to be someone, even in this remote place, whom she could trust. Perhaps the authorities would be less threatening here than they were at the Cairo airport.

Finally, after asking several street vendors, she found police headquarters on the road south of her hotel. An overhead fan squealed, trying without much success to move the dusty air above two battered wooden desks and the men sprawled comfortably in chairs behind them.

The younger man looked up and rose as she entered. "I am Lieutenant Mustafa Bey. How may I be of service, madam?"

The tall, broad-shouldered man's soulful eyes were bright with intelligence and curiosity. She found him very arresting, and hoped at last she could get some real help.

"I'm Olivia Cranston. I'm here looking for my brother, Dr. Charles Cranston."

"Forgive me. I should have seen immediately that you are Charlie's twin sister." Deep dimples creased his lean brown cheeks. "He speaks of you constantly."

Olivia took a ragged breath of relief. "Then, you know my brother. Have you any idea where I might find him?"

His smile vanished. "You are concerned, Miss Cranston? Charlie often goes off on little expeditions on his own. But I would suggest you inquire at Institute House. As you know, your brother works under Dr. Harris and it just so happens he has today returned to Luxor."

Something in Lieutenant Bey's tone as he spoke about Ford made her pause. "Do you know Dr. Harris well?" she asked, watching him closely.

Again dimples deepened in his cheeks. "We both went to Brown University in America. Ford and I were on the crew team together for four years."

She swallowed her disappointment, hoping it didn't show on her face. Trying to explain to this man the spiritual bond she shared with her brother that had propelled her on this mad chase, or asking him to believe his dear friend Ford was a thief would be an impossibility. So she was back to square one. On her own. Still looking for her brother, and now for Dr. Fordham Harris, too.

"I'll take your advice," she said softly and retreated once again, not liking failure any better the second time around.

As she slowly made her way back to the Winter Palace, the early-evening light reflected golden tones off the ancient stone. The hotel almost seemed to welcome her home.

Farita hovered anxiously at the entrance. Olivia knew the guide was waiting for her. But right this minute, with Charlie's whereabouts still unknown, she couldn't feel more than a trace of guilt. "I'm sorry, Farita, I just wanted a few minutes to explore on my own," she apologized, trying to forestall a scolding, however gentle it might be.

Relief made Farita appear even younger than her years. "I understand, Miss Cranston. But for your safety, from now on, please stay with the tour or allow me to arrange a personal escort for you."

"I promise I will," she said. She hated the lie, knowing she would leave the tour the instant she got an idea of where to find her brother. And if Ford bolted, she'd be right behind him. That is if he ever showed up, to begin with. But there was no point in worrying the young woman.

"Please, the others are in the dining room." Farita motioned her to follow.

"Is Dr. Harris here yet?" she tried to ask casually.

By Farita's lifted eyebrows, Olivia knew she'd failed. A sweet smile curved the guide's mouth. "I fear not, Miss Cranston. However, he shall arrive soon."

Farita's voice and expression spoke volumes; she thought Olivia had romantic inclinations toward the brilliant Dr. Harris. Actually, she could understand why Farita would jump to that conclusion. He was one of the handsomest men Olivia had ever met. Maybe it was his sheer ruggedness after the three-piece-suited mannequins she dealt with daily, but she didn't think so. It undoubtedly had more to do with the way the spark in his magnificent blue eyes could turn her insides to mush.

She'd never felt quite this way about a man before. She knew she couldn't trust him, yet he fascinated her, anyway. Her sense of self-preservation told her to stay away from him, but she couldn't. She had to keep a close watch in case he knew something about her brother. Yet, beyond necessity, she wondered if she wouldn't be drawn to his charismatic presence—and knew instinctively that she would.

Returning the guide's smile, Olivia shook her head. "I'm not very hungry, Farita. I'll just go up to my room."

"I will have a light supper sent to you. Please rest, Miss Cranston. We board the Emerald Empress at dawn."

Olivia's room was balmy, and a sweet-scented breeze wafted through the open window. As promised, a silver tray holding bottled water, hard flat bread, feta cheese and dates arrived. Suddenly ravenous, she ate everything and then set the empty tray out in the hall.

Even though she felt exhausted, she methodically carried out her nightly ritual—one hundred strokes of the brush through her hair before twisting it on top of her head, teeth next, vitamins, fifteen minutes of stretching and a warm bath. She caught herself falling asleep twice in the deep claw-footed tub before she decided enough was enough, grabbed up a large white towel that smelled faintly of jasmine and wrapped herself in it.

The sound of hooves on cobblestones drew her to the window. Below in the street, a horse-drawn carriage took a couple for a romantic drive along the Nile. She sighed, leaning against the window frame and watched them disappear from view. It would be nice to have someone with whom to share the romance of the Nile. Particularly if he were young and handsome, with sun-streaked hair and piercing blue eyes.

Where had that thought come from?

Olivia pressed her ear to the connecting wall between her room and Ford's. Obviously he hadn't returned yet. Where could he be? She couldn't shake the feeling it had something to do with Charlie. Why else would he be lying to her every step of the way?

Unlike her twin, Olivia didn't like to live dangerously, and Fordham I. Harris spelled D-A-N-G-E-R in capital letters. She might find Ford physically attractive but she wasn't the type of woman who would enjoy visiting her lover in jail—and that surely was where he was headed.

She turned from the wall, placed her towel carefully over a chair to dry and collapsed onto the bed. She pulled a light sheet over her body, determined to get a few minutes of peace. She guessed she would need every ounce of stamina to deal with Ford once he realized she was following him.

She closed her eyes, willing her mind to reach out for Charlie in the dark.

Nothing.

DARKNESS OBSCURED the uneven cobblestones of the narrow street leading to Institute House, but Ford knew the way by heart. A zig here and a zag there saved the Land Rover some bumps from the deep ruts. After bouncing all over tarnation to find a man named Omar, exhaustion made him fuzzy. He fumbled in his pocket for the compound gate key.

But the gate stood open, and beyond, lights burned in the front office window. Why would anyone be here at this hour?

Charlie?

A surge of adrenaline burned away his fatigue and he ran across the courtyard to throw open the door. Its bang echoed through the hallway.

His secretary and Moose looked around in surprise, a whisper of Olivia's name still hanging in the air between them.

"What has she done now?" Ford asked.

"I presume you mean Miss Cranston." Beatrice sniffed. "She interrupted my teatime today and quite persistently drilled me about her brother." She gave him a sly smile. "*And* you."

"She then found my office," Moose said, taking up the tale in a much calmer way, and flashing Beatrice a melting smile. "I suggested that she speak with you, but it appears you already know the problem."

"I'll leave you gentlemen to settle the matter of Miss Cranston. She's already made me late for my supper," Beatrice said, her back as straight as a drill sergeant's. "Good evening, Dr. Harris. Lieutenant Bey."

After she marched off, Moose grinned and perched himself on the edge of her desk. "I envy you your Miss Smyth. No one gets past her."

The niggling suspicion that had persisted all through his exasperating afternoon—that Olivia had capitulated too quickly—now became a crashing headache. He should have known better. After all, her twin was just as stubborn!

He threw himself into the uncomfortable chair behind Beatrice's desk. "What did Olivia try to get out of you?"

"Charlie's whereabouts." Moose gave him the same kind of quizzical look he used to flash before every crew race at Brown. "Ford, do you think it is wise to allow a woman that desirable to roam the streets of Luxor alone?"

"I thought I had it all arranged!" He pinched the bridge of his nose and closed his eyes for an instant. "I knew she had no intention of going back to Cairo, but I thought she'd at least stay at the hotel until I could find out what's going on."

"Where is Charlie, Ford?" The soft voice held a suggestion of anxiety.

Regret clamped like a vise around Ford's gut. He couldn't tell his best friend the whole truth; he couldn't take the chance. "I haven't seen or heard from him in over ten days." Jumping to his feet, he allowed Moose to see his own apprehension. "He came to me two months ago with a story Omar the digger tells. The legend passed down through Omar's family for hundreds of years is that some ancestor, probably a grave robber, found the tomb of Osiris. But, since he was being chased, he placed a priceless box containing Osiris's hand in a hiding place. He was to return for it later, but he died at the hands of his pursuers before he could give his son the exact location." Ford shook his head in exasperation. "Supposedly it's still there. Except no one knows where to begin looking."

"To believe this tale you must also believe that Osiris and Isis truly existed as humans, not merely as gods created by my people." Moose, son of one of Egypt's oldest and most powerful families, spoke softly, templing his fingers.

"I can't believe every legend I hear. There's one for every tomb and temple, you know." He got up and began to pace the worn oriental rug on the stone floor. "Charlie believes it, though. We had a big blowup about his theory. He stormed off on holiday, vowing to prove me and the rest of the archaeology world wrong. That was the last I saw of him."

Moose sucked in a deep breath.

"I found Omar today out preparing for the Institute excavation at the Valley city. He said the young Dr. Cranston visited him nine days ago and made him tell the legend again and again. That's the last sighting of the young fool."

Moose looked up warily. "There are rumors that an Osiris resurrection cult is practicing once again. My officers laugh, but the villagers are anxious to believe in something. This cult is not so benign—during dynastic Egypt, the members of this group believed immortality could be realized by participating in certain funerary rites."

Perspiration trickled in rivulets down Ford's back. The room was hot, but his temper was hotter. If he gave away too much, Moose would wade into this mess right beside him.

"Great!" he bellowed, not having to fake his anger. "All we need are a bunch of cult crazies to deal with!" Unfortunately, that was exactly what he feared.

Moose smiled, his dimples deep creases in his cheeks. "You forget, we also have Miss Cranston. She strikes me as a woman who is accustomed to getting her own way."

"Trust me, I haven't forgotten Olivia! Do me a favor, Moose. Keep an eye on her for me, will you? I need to be on the Emerald Empress tomorrow when it sails."

Moose pinned him with dark questioning eyes. "You're taking a cruise? Why?"

Steady as a rock, he held his friend's eyes. "It's business. We'll be back here at Karnak the day after. By then, I expect to know more about Charlie's whereabouts. Meanwhile, you stick to Olivia like wrappings on a mummy."

"Never fear. I shall not fail you." Moose turned and disappeared into the night, moving with the same graceful stride that had mesmerized every coed at Brown. Everything about Mustafa Bey, better known to his fraternity brothers and crew team as "the moose," might be of mammoth proportion, but his moves with women, Ford remembered, smiling, were finesse personified.

Ford headed back to the Winter Palace. He had to follow instructions and make an appearance on the Emerald Empress. Would there be an Interpol agent following along? He also wondered when the people hiding Charlie would contact him.

The desk clerk had his key ready. Jiggling it in his palm, Ford turned back. "Miss Cranston is all checked in, right?"

The clerk winked as a grin spread across his face. "Yes, sir. It is all taken care of."

Ford frowned as he headed for the elevator, worrying about the possible significance of the desk clerk's grin. What mischief had Olivia been up to?

By now, she must be asleep. He knew enough about the tour to anticipate the early-morning wake-up call. Confident all was well at least for tonight, he showered and fell into bed.

A sound woke him near dawn. Prying his lids wide open, he turned his head. A man stood silhouetted in the french doors. Heart thudding, Ford bounded off the bed, knocking over the lamp beside it.

"Get the hell out of here!" he roared, acting on instinct. *No!* This might be a contact. "Wait!"

But the man scampered out onto the balcony and jumped to the next porch. By the time Ford got outside, the intruder was disappearing through the open french doors of the next room.

A woman's scream ripped the night.

Ford didn't bother to look below for accomplices. All he could think of was that scream of terror. He forgot about the intruder and what his appearance might mean. He had to know if that woman was safe. He jumped to the ledge outside her window and pushed through the open doors.

He recognized the woman immediately. It was Olivia! She was sitting up in bed, in shock, her hair a curtain hiding her face. His mouth went dry at the fragile beauty her scantily clad form revealed. Only a silken nightgown covered her, loosely hugging the curves of her breasts and waist.

He slammed the hall door through which the man had escaped, knowing pursuit would be futile, then went to her. The instant he pulled Olivia into his arms, he realized her fierce embrace was pure reflex; she was still half-asleep. She felt fragile; her cheeks moist and hot, her hair a soft tickle against his stomach. He couldn't seem to catch his breath.

If he'd ever wanted anyone this much, he couldn't remember. Desire blotted out the danger, his need to protect her, his anxiety about her brother. Raw wanting dulled his usual caution.

He pressed soft silky kisses across her forehead and down her cheek, tasting salt. "Olivia, love, it's okay. I'm here."

She suddenly stiffened in his arms, and he knew beyond a doubt she had finally come fully awake.

"Don't call me that," she whispered. Her eyes glittered in her pale face, but to his surprise she remained calm, staring up at him. "I presume you're in my room because you heard my scream. It wasn't a nightmare, was it? Someone ran through my room. Were you chasing him, Ford? Why are you staying here? I know you have rooms at Institute House like the rest of the staff. What's going on?"

She was absolutely amazing! A stranger had vaulted through her window. Another stranger sat on her bed holding her, hard with desire, and she calmly analyzed the facts.

He was torn with indecision. How much could he safely tell her? His thoughts on the intruder were mere speculation, and he didn't want to alarm her unnecessarily. He was certain she wasn't as tough and indomitable as she saw herself.

"They're painting my quarters at Institute House, so I had to take a room in the hotel." He smiled to reassure her, deciding that until he found out who the hell was behind this mess, he wouldn't frighten her even more. "The guy tried to break into my room to rob me. I woke up and caught him in the act. He jumped onto your balcony and escaped."

A flush of color came over her face and neck, making her eyes look hard, like amethyst chips. She obviously didn't believe a word he'd said.

"I see. You'd better report the incident to the hotel and to your friend, Lieutenant Bey. As you can see, I'm fine."

Feisty. Self-possessed. And achingly beautiful. Why did she have to show up in Egypt now?

At another time, in another place, he'd never leave her. Instead, he took the only course of action open to him. "Listen, Olivia, I'll be gone tomorrow, looking for Charlie out in the desert. Promise you'll stay here, in the hotel, until I contact you."

"Don't worry, Ford. I know I'll be hearing from you soon. Now, don't you think you'd better report this?"

He hesitated. His eyes searched her face, reading the suspicion and longing warring in her eyes.

Reluctantly, he got up to leave. He locked the balcony door securely and turned back to the bed. She sat straight up, her hands pulling the sheet up to mask what little covering her silky negligee afforded.

"You'll be hearing from me again sooner than you think," Ford assured her.

Double-checking the lock, he disappeared out her door, barely catching her whispered, "I know."

The hotel corridor, dimly lit by wall sconces, was peaceful. No one else appeared to have been disturbed. Unseen, he slipped into his room.

He stopped short. Smack in the middle of his pillow lay a note. The brief message held no pretension—just instructions:

"Tomorrow at the Temple of Hathor. In the Osiris Chamber."

Chapter Four

The sheet bunched around Olivia's thighs, twisting and trapping her as she tossed and turned on her pillow.

A shrill ring jarred through her, forcing her awake. She groped for the phone, squinting into the thin streak of sunlight falling across her face. A cheery voice informed her that a continental breakfast would be served to the tour group and that her luggage should be outside her door in thirty minutes.

Every muscle in her body ached. For hours after Ford had left her alone in the dark, she'd fought with herself. And, even now, after her brain felt muzzy from trying to rationalize her reaction to waking up in his arms, she could still feel his strength and breathe in the clean soapy scent of his skin.

Shouldn't she have been surprised, at the very least, to come fully awake in his arms? Panic-stricken?

Instead, she'd felt desire. Maybe she wasn't as immune to dangerous men as she'd thought.

She sat up and stretched, staring at her reflection in the mirror, surprised to find she didn't look any different. She *felt* different.

She had to find out what was going on. Her intuition might tell her Ford was no ordinary thief, that he wouldn't weave these elaborate lies unless he had a very good reason; but could she trust intuition when she felt this extraordinary attraction to him?

Somehow she had to find concrete evidence that would show whether or not Ford was connected to her brother's disappearance.

She pressed her ear to the wall and heard his shower running. Without a second thought, she slipped into her silk robe. Now was her best chance to catch him off guard.

She peered into the corridor, noting the used coffee tray outside Ford's room. She slipped down the hall, fear mingling with excitement as she reached for his doorknob. It turned easily in her hand. Lucky for her, he must have neglected to lock his door after putting his breakfast tray in the hallway.

At the last second, she had an attack of conscience. She really shouldn't... but Charlie was more important to her than shoulds or coulds. Her heart in her throat, she pushed the door open. If he caught her, she'd pretend she'd come to thank him for last night.

His sheets were a tumbled mess and his clothes were strewn all over the place. Just like a man! She wasn't sure what she was looking for, but she rifled through his black tote, anyway. Her quick search yielded only underwear, socks and two polo shirts. On the dresser, loose change and a thin wallet with identification and some Egyptian money revealed no secrets. A pair of black jeans and a white shirt hung over one chair. She thrust her hand into a pocket of the jeans and pulled out a folded piece of paper.

The water stopped. In the sudden silence, she sucked in a sharp breath in response to her last-minute find. She glanced quickly at the paper before jamming it back into his jeans and sprinting for the door. She shot into her own room and slammed her door.

Her heart pounding, she pressed herself against the connecting wall to his room, listening for sounds that he had noticed anything amiss. Damn the man, he was actually whistling!

The Osiris Chamber in the Temple of Hathor.

The words meant nothing to her. She splashed cold water on her face, pulled her clothes for the day out of her bag and set the luggage in the hall. Time was against her now. Midway through her sketchy ablutions, a thought struck her. She raced to her purse and pulled out the itinerary. The Empress was sailing to Hathor's Temple today.

Maybe that was why Ford was taking this cruise—to get to the temple. A deep resolve settled into her soul; she wasn't going to let him out of her sight. No matter what, she would find Charlie; regardless of earthquakes, a baffling trail or Dr. Fordham I. Harris himself.

She dressed in one of her own designs, a white, black and red jumpsuit from last season, and presented herself for breakfast right on time.

The rest of the group, except for Ford, were already present in the sitting room chatting together. She took one look at the buffet choices: runny eggs, unrecognizable sausages, lumpy yogurt, and decided she'd stick to coffee. Thick and bitter, it required two spoonfuls of sugar, making it only marginally palatable. She sipped tentatively and asked the waiter to bring her some bottled water, noticing that everyone else had a plastic container at their place.

"Drink tea, my dear. So much more civilized." Irmentrude sniffed as only the English do, making it sound as if she were quoting the queen.

Olivia turned to find both the British matron and her sulky nephew standing behind her, observing the tour group with some skepticism.

"Stephen and I would be pleased for you to join us at meals during the trip. Traveling alone can be deuced lonely."

Irmentrude was the quintessence of solid respectability, even if her nephew seemed a boor. Although Olivia was tired and preoccupied, she couldn't be rude to the older woman.

"Thank you. That's very kind of you."

"Jolly good show, then!" Irmentrude rammed her pith helmet over her short gray hair, while Stephen winced at her boisterousness. "It appears Farita is ready for us."

Farita's lovely smile lit the whole room. And, to Olivia's surprise, Gameel Mujod entered behind her.

"Ladies and gentlemen, I am honored to introduce Mr. Mujod, president of the Mujod Tours, who will accompany us on our journey up the Nile." Her soft voice held a note of awe.

Self-importance twitched across his face as Mr. Mujod bowed to the tour members, fully aware of the honor he was doing them. "I hope your memories of Luxor are happy ones." His small eyes refused to single out any one person, settling instead on a spot high above everyone's heads. "Please, now we will walk across the corniche to the Emerald Empress where

Mujod Tours is honored to present an unexpected and much-desired addition to our group."

Olivia knew exactly what desirable addition would be on board. She couldn't wait to find out what his reaction would be when he realized she had followed him.

Other ships anchored along the dock paled beside the Emerald Empress. She gleamed the brightest, with three rows of oblong windows glistening in the sunshine. On board, the patina of old wood, lovingly cared for, and shiny brass, greeted them as they entered the registration lounge. Two uniformed men stood at attention behind an intricately carved counter.

"Please, all formalities have been completed. After you have visited your cabin, join us upstairs in the main salon," Mr. Mujod said.

They all hurried along, urged on by the little man's air of excitement. Farita called out names and one of the men behind the counter handed each tour member a key, a pass to be used when reboarding the ship and then pointed out what level their cabins were located on.

Olivia's three pieces of luggage sat neatly side by side in a compact but lavishly decorated room on the bottom level. The Nile lapped against the hull a few feet beneath her window, but she couldn't discern any movement. She was grateful to have a modern bathroom to herself, even if it was the size of a postage stamp and contained no bathtub, only the narrowest shower stall she'd ever seen.

Anxious to make sure Ford was actually on board, where he couldn't elude her, Olivia lost no time in ascending the beautiful wooden staircase. On the second level, a sitting room with an overstuffed brocade settee and coffee table obscured the view of the darkened dining room. She continued to the top level where a large salon with an ornate wooden bar at one end and a dance floor at the other seemed to serve as the main gathering area. Double glass doors led to the partially covered outside deck; its antique wicker chairs, love seats and lounges looked particularly inviting.

Irmentrude waved her over and Olivia settled at one end of a green velvet couch. The furniture and ambience could have come straight out of an Agatha Christie novel. The four ladies from Indiana buzzed excitedly in the furniture grouping directly behind her. Across the aisle, Stephen and Marta had managed to sit just close enough that no one could get between them, yet far enough that they didn't have to speak to each other. In comparison, Lois and Ray looked nearly bug-eyed with anticipation.

"I adore surprises," Lois said, greeting her warmly, her tanned face crinkling as she laughed. "What do you think they have planned for us?"

Before Olivia could tell her, Mr. Mujod appeared at the top of the impressive staircase. Directly behind him stood Ford. They began to ascend, until they stood in the lounge.

The low noises of the salon were all around her. At the back of the room, a small group of French tourists were asking questions of their guide and interpreter. Next to them, a smaller group of Italians were doing the same. Waiters passed cups of coffee and tea. Farita hovered over her group like a mother hen, making sure everyone had what they needed.

Olivia was aware of everything and everyone around her. But, for just an instant, she concentrated only on Ford—remembering his body heat and inhaling his scent. She blinked, unable to understand her reaction, which made her go hot and cold at the same time.

After his first shocked recognition, Ford smiled directly at her as if they shared something clever and amusing, something no one else could understand. Then his eyes darkened, and she could tell that he, too, was remembering their brief but extremely intimate embrace of the night before.

She refused to blush like a teenager. So, he'd seen her in her nightgown. He hadn't had much on, either, at the time. Again, unbidden, the feel of his exposed chest rose to haunt her. She shook her head, as if by the very action she could clear her thoughts.

Despite everything, he was still her best and only link to her brother, she rationalized. If he couldn't help her find Charlie, no one could. Deliberately flipping her heavy hair over one shoulder, she smiled back at him.

He folded his arms over his chest in a relaxed picture of amazing self-confidence and composure.

"Ladies and gentlemen, it is my very great honor to introduce the renowned archaeologist, Dr. Fordham Harris, who has so generously agreed to accompany us on our Nile journey. Dr. Harris will share with us his expertise on the temples we shall visit. This is an occasion of great honor for all of us." With a grand flourishing gesture, Mr. Mujod backed away, giving Ford center stage.

He walked to the middle of the room, offering a greeting in French and Italian to the other groups, and somehow ended up standing only two feet from her.

"Good morning."

His smile made every woman in the room sit up a little straighter, including Irmentrude. Marta leaned forward, her green eyes narrowing into slits. Beside her, Stephen frowned.

"There is nowhere else on earth like the land of Egypt," he said. "Every time I venture into a temple, I experience a profound sense of awe. This culture was, in a real sense, the beginning of western civilization."

He moved closer to her and she could feel his startling charisma reaching out to capture, not only her, but everyone in the tour group. His hand brushed the back of her couch, nearly touching her hair. She could barely breathe, let alone concentrate on what the man had to say.

"Dendera is a small village sixty kilometers north of Luxor on the west bank of the Nile. The temple there is sacred to the Egyptian goddess of love, joy and beauty, Hathor, who was depicted in many forms," Ford said. "As a woman with two horns and a sun disk, as a woman with a cow's head bearing the sun disk and horns and as a woman's head with cow's ears, a compromise of the other two."

Warning bells went off in Olivia's head. Could the note she'd taken such desperate measures to see be perfectly innocent? Perhaps it had only been a reminder of some kind for his talk to the tour group. She forced herself to concentrate on everything Ford had to say. Maybe he would slip up somehow, giving himself away...or maybe he would prove to be perfectly innocent.

"Hathor was worshiped at Dendera, and her consort, Horus, the son of Isis and Osiris, at Edfu. The temples at these sites face each other, and are the only ones in Egypt that do not look to the Nile, the life-giver."

Olivia's mind focused on one name—Osiris! *The Osiris Chamber at the Temple of Hathor.* Could there be a clue in the chamber at the temple? Charlie himself? Confusion and rising excitement battled within her. She leaned forward as Ford moved away to the front of the room, paused dramatically, then turned to face his audience.

"To understand the monuments, you must understand the gods and goddesses of Egypt. Primarily Osiris and Isis."

Several people in the room nodded as if they knew what he was talking about. Olivia wished she were among the initiated. Charlie had mentioned Osiris over and over again in his correspondence. And the note had directed Ford to the Osiris Chamber, whatever that was.

"Legend has it that Osiris was the earliest king of Egypt. It is told that he brought the Egyptians out of savagery, giving them laws and teaching them how to cultivate the land. He married his sister, Isis, and their wise and benevolent rule was praised by gods and men alike. But Osiris's jealous twin brother, Set, murdered the king and dismembered his body into fourteen pieces, scattering the parts throughout Egypt."

Ford reacted to the collective gasp by lowering his voice in a dramatic gesture she found charming and completely captivating.

"Isis searched the land, and each time she found a part of Osiris, she erected a shrine and marked the spot with a tamarisk tree to signify that Osiris had risen from the dead. But she never found his left hand. In order for him to attain immortality, she made a gold replica of the hand and buried it secretly. Her devoted lamentations so moved the gods that they restored Osiris and made him ruler over the land of the dead. The son of the royal pair, Horus, defeated his wicked uncle, Set, in bloody hand-to-hand combat and regained the throne."

A loud burst of applause made Ford laugh. "Quite a legend, isn't it! Any questions so far?"

Patty's hand shot up. "Wasn't there some cult connected to Osiris?"

"Yes." Ford nodded, all trace of his smile gone. "Osiris became the focus of a resurrection cult in dynastic Egypt, whose worshipers believed that by practicing certain rites, they could attain life after death."

"Is there not a theory put forth by some scholars that Osiris and Isis were in fact living individuals, not gods?"

The shock of hearing the usually speechless Freya, the South African woman, utter a syllable brought the entire group to bemused attention, with the exception of her daughter, Marta, who seemed to be trying to disappear into her chair.

"In point of fact, is there not a theory that the body parts of Osiris, along with priceless treasures, are still to be found where Isis buried them?'' Freya continued in her curiously flat voice.

''Most of the traditional sites have been excavated, to no purpose. But I am certain that there are many who *want* to believe in buried treasure,'' Ford drawled, obviously trying to dampen any such expectations in this group. Clearly, he didn't hold with this superstition, nor did he think highly of people, especially scientists, who did.

Olivia could sense Ford struggle with himself, then finally give in and glance toward her. In that one cryptic look, a piece of the puzzle fell into place.

Charlie was one of those scholars Ford curled his lip at! Could her brilliant, headstrong brother really only be off on nothing more dangerous than a treasure hunt? And she'd trekked halfway across the globe because she'd sensed he needed her! Of course, that still wouldn't explain Ford's secretive behavior, or why he had stolen the amulet, unless he was taking advantage of Charlie's absence to cast suspicion on him.

A thousand unanswered questions roared through her ears, causing her to miss the rest of the comments. The next thing she knew, Farita had them all up and moving toward the dining room.

The room was beautifully appointed with rich wood paneling, lit by genuine Tiffany lamps. Ford had conveniently disappeared and Olivia found herself ensconced at a huge oval table surrounded by the rest of her tour group. A plate, piled high with food, was served. Only a small mound of plain rice was recognizable. Egypt, she decided, would be good for her diet if not her peace of mind.

The minute she could escape, she rushed back to the lounge but found it empty. The ship wasn't that large and she was determined to find Ford. He wasn't on deck, or anywhere that she could see. Desperate, she inquired at the registration desk.

"Dr. Harris is housed in the owner's suite." This young man gave her the same kind of coy look as the desk clerk at the Winter Palace had. Before this nonsense ended, all of Egypt would think she was shamelessly pursuing the elusive Dr. Harris.

"However, Dr. Harris has already gone ashore," the crewman continued in the same silky voice.

The ship traveled so smoothly on the serene Nile, she hadn't realized they were stopped. She had just enough time to rush to her cabin for her bag before the tour disembarked for the temple.

At Dendera, site of the temple of Hathor, heaps of mud bricks made up an enclosure wall that completely encircled several stone buildings in the complex. Outside the imposing temple facade, Farita handed out very small, very powerful flashlights, compliments of Mujod Tours.

The moment Olivia entered through the huge doors, she understood why they'd been given the flashlights. Everyone stopped, allowing their eyes to adjust to the play of shadows and filtered light. Finally, she could make out a forest of columns, but ahead, the depths of the temple were even darker.

Suddenly, that odd feeling of being watched made Olivia look behind her. As if on cue, Ford stepped into the broad beam of sunlight that illuminated the floor a few feet from the doorway. He seemed larger than life.

"Welcome to the Pronaos of Dendera. After the decline of the ancient Egyptian religion, the Coptics inhabited this site, desecrating the great carvings, covering the ceiling with soot from their cooking fires." Ford strode into the very center of the room, his forceful voice sounding even deeper, more mesmerizing as it echoed in the shadowy depths leading off from both sides of the hall.

He led them through the Hall of Offerings to the west corridor, which was richly decorated with reliefs.

"We are in one of the twin chapels of Osiris. Look up," he commanded. "Behold the famous Zodiac of Dendera."

Everyone gasped in admiration. The intricate stone etchings showed the goddess, Nut, with her fingers and toes stretching out and touching the world at four points, her slender body arching, forming the vault of heaven. Beneath the goddess were the six northern signs of the Egyptian zodiac. In the next room a similar figure of the goddess hovered over the remaining six signs of the zodiac.

"This zodiac was cut from the roof and placed in the Bibliothèque Nationale in Paris. What you see is a mold of the original. Countless priceless Egyptian treasures were taken out of the country and are now in private collections or museums all over the world."

The faint edge of disgust in Ford's voice drew a plethora of questions. He should know all about stolen treasures, Olivia fumed silently, angry with herself for her fascination with him.

While he answered all the questions the group threw at him, she slipped away to a smaller room where the dark was completely blinding. She took out her guidebook and concentrated her tiny beam of light on the text. She seemed to be in a room that represented the tomb of Osiris. Excitement curled along her skin. Could this be the room mentioned in the note?

She flashed her light around the walls, curious. Her artist's eye had begun to make some sense out of the wall scenes, obviously resurrection motifs. And everywhere were the peculiar cartouches—ovals enclosing the symbols for a sovereign's name. She played her light along the ceiling.

She didn't really know what she was looking for. But there must be some reason the note instructed Ford to come into this room. Methodically she searched the walls, playing her light up and down, frustrated. And all the while, she could hear Ford's voice lecturing nearby.

She moved toward the doorway she'd come through, not wanting to lose sight of him. He'd come on this tour for a specific reason, and come hell or high water, she was going to find out what it was.

Ford finished and the group split up, each person going their own way to explore, after Farita gave them strict instructions to be at the front of the temple in a half hour. Catching a glimpse of Ford's sun-lightened hair moving away from the rest, she followed him. By now her eyes had adjusted to the darkness and she felt comfortable in the black shifting shadows.

As she ducked in and out of chamber after chamber, checking every so often to make sure Ford was just ahead, she saw no one else from the group. Obviously she was way off the beaten track. Then, out of the corner of her eye, she glimpsed Marta and Stephen, whispering, hidden together behind a pillar. They glanced up and made a sound similar to a groan. Embarrassed at stumbling onto the site of their tryst, she turned to leave them their privacy.

Farita materialized out of the shadows, blocking her way, and Olivia gasped in fear.

The guide glanced over her shoulder at the guilty pair. "I believe your parents are looking for you, Marta."

The young blond woman ran past them, followed slowly by Stephen, who threw them a cheeky grin.

"I am sorry if I frightened you, Olivia, but I must caution you about your shoulder bag. I thought I glimpsed someone lurking in the shadows," Farita said softly.

"Here?" Olivia glanced around. "I hadn't noticed anyone or anything out of line."

"I apologize again. In this light it is difficult to see correctly. Please do be careful. Unfortunately, we are not a rich nation."

"I understand." As if to demonstrate, Olivia shifted her small black shoulder bag over her head for security.

"Good." Farita smiled and nodded. "Come. We must leave in five minutes."

"That's all I need to complete some motifs I've been sketching. I'll meet you at the front door," Olivia said, already heading toward the place she'd last seen Ford. Surely he had been heading for the chapel the guidebook showed at the back of the temple.

In a moment she found herself in profound darkness; no sound penetrated this remote area. Gradually, she became aware of the sound of her own breathing. Where could Ford have gotten to?

Concentrating hard, she tried to get some sense of Charlie's being in this place once—some idea of what he might have seen or felt.

Nothing.

Frustrated, she swung her light wildly about the chapel. A shadowy silhouette flickered across the wall and hot fear stopped Olivia's heart. She blinked and the shadow was gone. Telling herself it must have been her imagination, she forced her body to begin breathing again, although her pulse still raced.

She stepped closer to the back wall, where a depiction of the shrine of Osiris was painted. The god was seated on a throne to judge the dead, his face dominated by his oddly shaped white crown. She tried to interpret the inscriptions below, taking them line by line. In the short time she had been studying them, she could already recognize some of the symbols.

She began to feel vaguely uncomfortable, here, alone in the dark, but refused to give in to superstition. Defiantly, she swept her light over the ceiling, but could see nothing that interested her.

Behind her, something shuffled across the stone floor. Her only coherent thought was that she could use her flashlight as a weapon. She jumped up, whirling, and gasped.

She would have smacked Ford full in the face if he hadn't ducked just in time. His arms coiled around her. She let out a loud yelp and tried to free herself, but he just held her tighter.

"What the hell are you doing here?" he said through taut lips.

She struggled to free herself. Reluctantly, he loosened his grip, yet didn't completely release her.

"What am *I* doing here? You mean, what are *you* doing here? You said you would look for my brother!"

She flashed her light into his face. He was frowning. Yet she immediately became aware of his hands stroking up and down her back, his fingertips pressing against every sensitive nerve ending along her spine. What was he up to this time? Which mood would it be, charming or brusque?

"*You* were supposed to wait for me, back at the Winter Palace. You shouldn't be wandering around all alone, Olivia."

Steeling herself against the insidious sensual caress of his hands, she glared at him. "Don't you think it's about time you leveled with me about Charlie?"

He pushed her flashlight away from his eyes and it fell from her nerveless fingers, dropping to the floor. Suddenly, he bent his head and kissed the top of her nose.

Charm again! Her defenses kicked in and she jerked away from him. "I demand to know where my brother is! The truth, for once."

Ford glanced around, swooped down to retrieve her flashlight and dragged her toward the entrance. "Let's go. Our time here is up. We can talk on the ship, if you'll come to my cabin before dinner."

She felt his anger in his tight grip on her hand and the way his eyes hardened as they searched the corridors. Good! She could deal with his anger a lot easier than his charm.

FORD TRIED to cover his frustration on the way back to the ship by speculating who his contact might be. If Olivia kept following him everywhere, she'd scare off whoever was trying to approach him. Somehow, he had to make her stay away.

He stared at her resolute profile. Even two rows ahead of him, he could see her delicate chin lifted in determination. He'd recognized it the first day he laid eyes on her, even Moose had seen it. The lady always got her own way.

Well, not this time. This time she was going to have to back off. If she knew what was at stake, she'd cooperate—should he tell her?

The temptation was strong. But it wouldn't be a wise decision. There was no way he could get anyone else involved, not until he knew for sure where Charlie was—and, more important, whether he was working in tandem with those crazy cult people who would use him for his knowledge of Osiris and his ability to get his hands on artifacts they considered necessary to their lunatic activities. Until then, it would be too risky. He'd just have to think of something else to appease Olivia in the meantime.

As soon as the van stopped dockside, he surged to his feet and walked toward the phone shack about a half mile away. Maybe he should contact Moose and let him know what was going on. By the time he'd decided against that idea, too, about a half hour had elapsed.

He returned to the boat. The opulence of the owner's suite brought a smile to his face. The place, with its rich mahogany walls and brass sconces, reminded Ford of a wealthy Englishmen's club. Mujod had gone all out for him. Ford found this special treatment embarrassing, though just maybe it could be put to good use.

Unbuttoning his shirt, he stalked into the bedroom. He stopped in surprise when he saw what awaited him on his bed. In the middle of the bed was a rough drawing, the cream-colored vellum paper from his own desk a stark contrast against the deep burgundy spread. He stared blankly for a moment at the sketched falcon before he remembered it was the symbol for the god Horus. So, he'd have to wait to meet his contact at Edfu, where Horus's temple was located. That should give him enough time to scare Olivia off, so she wouldn't interrupt his business again.

But how in the hell had this message gotten into his room? He raced down the steps to the registration desk before the clerk who had been there all day could go off duty.

"Can you tell me if anyone else besides the passengers and crew have been aboard today?"

The young man behind the desk stiffened to attention. "No one may come on this ship without a boarding pass."

"Are you certain there was no one else on this ship today but the rightful passengers and crew?"

His interrogation caught the attention of two officers coming down the stairs.

"Is there a problem, Dr. Harris?" The purser stepped forward. "I personally supervised the gangway while we were docked at Dendera."

Ford stared into the man's solemn eyes for a long minute before he shook his head. "No problem.

However, I'd like to check on the timing of the other tours. What about the Italian group?''

"They left before the English-speaking tour and are not back yet. And the French left a few minutes after you and aren't expected to return until late this evening.''

"Thank you.'' That seemed to rule out both those groups as candidates for his contact. How could any of them have known the meeting wasn't made at Dendera and gotten back to the ship before him in time to put the note on his bed.

Ford walked slowly up to his rooms, trying to absorb this latest twist. He wished he knew whether the person he was supposed to meet had Charlie, or merely more instructions. Either way, he was fairly sure now that there was a cult member on board. He passed Irmentrude and Stephen on the stairs and stared after them with new eyes. The four ladies from Indiana who sat talking together in the lounge no longer seemed so innocent.

He knew an Interpol agent had to be lurking around somewhere, too. He'd wondered why they hadn't made contact as they had promised after he told them about the cult. Were they watching him for leads? He'd have to be extra careful. The last thing he needed was for Interpol to interrupt his next chance for contact with Charlie's captors!

His shirt was off when Olivia's brisk knock sounded on his door. Automatically, he reached for it, then thought better of it and answered the door just as he was.

Compulsion sizzled through his blood as she slipped past him into the cabin. She'd decided to live dangerously tonight. She wore a red dress that looked to be no more than a slip. The silky material just brushed her curves, promising without being obvious. And it gave him one hell of an idea.

She closed the door behind her and glanced around at the opulent suite, looking surprised. Her lips curled into a tiny smile. "It's beautiful."

"You're beautiful." He altered his voice subtly, intent on frightening her away for good.

She flushed, all of her. The bare skin exposed by the daring dress couldn't be disguised. "Even though I don't have cow's ears?"

Until this moment, he hadn't guessed she possessed a sense of humor. He laughed despite the ache in his gut, the regret for what he was about to do, and moved closer.

She backed away and then stopped herself, stiffening, as if to take command again and deny that she'd shown a glimmer of weakness.

"Ford, are you prepared to tell me the truth now?" she asked, looking more beautiful than ever.

Something Ford had never felt before leaped up in response. "Yeah, there is one important thing you should know." He pulled her into his arms and kissed her slowly, opening her mouth with his tongue. She tasted exotic and so hot he couldn't keep from moving his hands over her body, feeling her shape through the thin silk.

"Stop!" Pulling her mouth away, breathing a little heavier, she backed halfway across the room. "I prefer your anger to your charm! You know how concerned I am about Charlie. Why are you lying to me?"

He couldn't do it. Maybe a half truth would work just as well.

"Because you're not helping Charlie by blundering all over Egypt trying to find him. Let me handle it my way." He forced his voice to be even and normal, trying to do the same to his pulse.

She looked startled. Something surfaced on her face for a moment, a faraway look he couldn't interpret. "You don't know where he is, do you, Ford?"

Gazing into her determined face, he knew nothing would stop her. Not his anger, or his attempt to charm her into complacency.

"What do you want from me, Olivia?"

The intense look she turned on him made the hairs on the back of his neck feel electrified.

"I want you to let me help you."

He jammed his hands into his pockets, feeling the amulet he'd hoped to trade at Dendera today. "How do you expect to do that?"

She threw up her head in the gesture he was coming to know all too well. "Let me into Charlie's rooms at Institute House in Luxor. Maybe I'll get some sense of him. Some idea where he went and why."

An idea clicked into place. If he could get her off the ship, strand her in Luxor, she couldn't make the journey upriver to Horus's temple at Edfu. She wouldn't get in his way or be in any particular danger. The plan appealed to him, even though he knew she'd be hopping mad.

Pleased with himself, he smiled. "Okay. I know about your twin telepathy thing. You've got yourself a deal. Tomorrow I'll take you ashore to Institute House."

Chapter Five

Olivia stared out her cabin window at the romantic picture Luxor made, stretching along the banks of the Nile like an image on a postcard. How could it look so peaceful, so idyllic, when her brother was missing?

Ford had promised to take her to Institute House today. Depending on what she found there, she'd decide how to handle the incriminating evidence she had against him.

He was a hard man to understand. One minute he was concerned, charismatic, caring; the next, indifferent and dismissive. And for just a moment last night, Olivia thought he was deliberately trying to scare her off with some sort of seduction routine. If that was his intent, it had backfired. But she had to admit, she was eager to see him, to find out which personality would emerge today.

There was a hard knock on her door, presumptuous and demanding. If he was in a cantankerous mood, she'd have no trouble dealing with him. He might be brilliant and undeniably sensual, but he was no match for her when she had her wits about her.

She yanked the door open and found his hand raised to knock again. Two could play at this game.

"Are you taking me to Institute House or not?"

He gave a nod of approval at her businesslike tone. "I always keep my promises. Let's go."

She walked silently beside him, easily keeping pace with his long strides until they reached a narrow cobblestone street. Then her footwork required all her diligence. They turned a corner and entered the street bazaar. Most of the tour was here, souvenir hunting on one of their few free days.

Ford tightened his grip on her hand and groaned when he saw the others. He quickened his pace but that didn't stop various members of the group from rushing up to ask his opinion or advice. They seemed to feel Ford was their personal resource.

He was surprisingly gracious, although he never slowed a step. Lois and Ray emerged from a linen shop and kept pace beside them halfway through the bazaar until some brass lanterns caught Lois's eye and she pulled her husband into the colorful stall.

Olivia felt his obvious relief, and then the ladies from Indiana stopped them to ask directions to the Temple of Luxor. Ford gave them the information, watched as they rushed off and then he turned to her. "Here, let's get out of this mess."

Irmentrude, with Stephen trailing dutifully behind her, caught up to them just as they turned into the twisting street leading to the Institute. She began to think the intrusions would never end.

"Jolly good show to find you here, Dr. Harris." Irmentrude's deep-set eyes squinted in the bright sunlight. "I didn't wish to mention this earlier, however I can't help being curious about what you think of the recent rash of burglaries of Egyptian artifacts from private collections."

"I wasn't aware that there had been more than two. But I believe other art pieces besides Egyptian items were also stolen. I think it's merely a sign of our times."

Ford's tension was obvious from the rigid set of his shoulders. Given what she knew about him, Olivia understood his reaction.

"I told you those mystery books you read are making you daffy! Come along, Aunt Irmie, it's time for a spot of tea." The usually comatose Stephen suddenly came to life, dragging his aunt toward a restaurant with outdoor seating.

Olivia glimpsed Marta trailing after her parents into the same coffeehouse. That would explain Stephen's eagerness.

Ford led her through the Institute's courtyard to a side door she hadn't noticed before. They totally bypassed the reception area. At the top of a narrow flight of stairs, he stopped.

"This is Charlie's room." He pushed the door open, allowing her to enter first.

In this part of the house the ceilings were low, which made the ancient tester bed look immense. She recognized Charlie's slippers tucked beneath a wide dresser at the edge of a worn persian carpet. The wide floorboards squeaked as she crossed to the desk under the window.

"Have you gone through all these papers? His desk at home never looked this neat."

Instantly he came to stare over her shoulder. "I went through them, but I didn't leave it this neat, either."

"Maybe a cleaning person straightened up," she said, whispering for no apparent reason. Sifting through the neat stacks of papers and notebooks, she watched Ford's face harden and a nerve throb along his jawline.

"Precisely what are you looking for, Olivia?"

The air conditioner was turned low, making the air heat-heavy; exactly the way his voice sounded.

"What were *you* looking for, Ford?"

He stood silhouetted in the small square window, staring at her, his irises darkening. She could definitely get lost in those eyes.

"For a clue that might tell where he was heading when he left here two weeks ago."

His desk drawers were a jumble, typically Charlie, but they revealed nothing. Finding the letters she'd written him bound in a rubber band made tears burn behind her lids. For a moment, she thought she might lose it—right here in front of Ford. Instead, she gripped her hands together and lifted her chin in defiance. Now was not the time for despair.

Through rapidly blinking eyes, she glimpsed a tiny kitchen hidden behind a half-closed curtain. From out of the blue a memory made her laugh outright, startling Ford. The bond she shared with Charlie might be weakening, but she'd never forget this!

Ford followed her, curious about her sudden change of mood. Olivia could barely maneuver around him to open the small refrigerator door and the even tinier freezer compartment so coated with frost that there was barely room for three small packages of food and a tray of ice cubes.

"What are you doing?" He loomed over her shoulder as she pried the freezer paper off the first package, which contained some unknown meat she refused to speculate on.

"If you're hungry, I'll buy you lunch."

Ignoring his sarcasm, she peeled back the paper from the second package. "Ta-da!" She thrust the package in Ford's face. Between the plastic wrap around the meat and the packaging were a few precious scraps of paper covered with Charlie's scrawl.

Ford snatched the package from her hands and stalked back to the light filtering in from the window. "How did you know this was there?"

"When we were kids, we used to play spy. Our parents were the bad guys and the freezer was our favorite place to leave our communiqués. We liked to see how long it would take them to find our notes."

The third package yielded two more sheets. She left the meat thawing on the counter, went over to the window and tried to peer over Ford's shoulder.

He shifted so she couldn't see.

She moved again. So did he.

"Let me see that!" she demanded as she yanked hard on his arm. She might not be an archaeologist or an Egyptian scholar, but she knew her brother best.

He thrust the papers at her and she spread the sheets out on the desk and pored over them, trying to make some sense of Charlie's garbled information. There was no way to tell in what order they should go, although she was careful to keep the sheets from the two different packages separate.

"Charlie is looking for the box with Osiris's hand, isn't he?"

"More fool he," Ford said, his voice heavy with sarcasm.

She hadn't looked at Ford when she asked the question, and she didn't now. "This—thet amulet—mentioned here..." She pointed to the place Charlie had written it in his notes. "It was stolen from the museum recently, wasn't it?"

He turned away, a sure sign of his guilt. "Yes. And so was the block of stone containing a portion of the Book of the Dead."

She leaned over the desk, spreading her hands protectively over Charlie's notes, trying to read Ford's face. His eyes were camouflaged by his thick lashes.

"It looks like Charlie was compiling some ancient instructions for something."

She saw the muscles in his strong throat contract all the way down to his chest where his shirt lay open and knew she'd hit on the truth. He squeezed his eyes shut and shook his head before admitting, "It's part of the ancient formula to resurrect Osiris. I didn't know until this moment what talismans were needed."

She looked at him for a long moment, feeling as if she'd swallowed a rock. "What?"

"It looks as if Charlie's done the work of a lifetime, sorting through the ancient wall carvings, studying the texts and the paintings to come up with such a detailed list. The amulet, a statue of Ament, the crown and collar Isis wore when she..." Suddenly he stopped.

He hesitated, then walked around the desk and took her hand in his. "No more." He was deadly serious. "Go back to Cairo. Now."

She'd almost duped him into telling her more of the truth than he wanted to. He stared at her, a look of utter frustration on his face. For one instant, Olivia felt so confused she couldn't think straight. "Don't you think it's time we leveled with each other?" she finally gasped out through her tight, dry throat.

Outside in the hall a floorboard squeaked one second before the door swung open to reveal Ford's hatchet-faced secretary. She looked none too pleased to see Olivia so cozy with her boss.

"I thought I heard voices up here. I see you found Dr. Harris, Miss Cranston." Her mouth pursed as she focused on Ford. "Lieutenant Bey is here to see you. I showed him into your office and served him tea. I expected you earlier, Dr. Harris."

The way she peered at Olivia over the top of her glasses left no doubt at whose feet she laid Ford's tardiness.

Ford scooped up the papers on the desk before Olivia could think to protest and hustled her through the door. "Could you bring another teacup, please, Beatrice?" He threw one of his dazzling smiles over his shoulder as he propelled Olivia through the corridor and down a wide staircase to his office.

Abandoning her for a moment, he went to his desk, and buried Charlie's papers in the mess littering the surface. Olivia glanced around; the sheer chaos of this room was staggering. Stacks of papers, jumbles of rocks, broken pieces of pottery and piles of thick dusty books covered every flat surface. She shuddered.

Ford grinned at her obvious discomfiture. "You know archaeologists. We spend our lives meticulously shifting dust centimeter by centimeter. So we allow ourselves the luxury of not being so tidy off the big site."

"Do not worry, Miss Cranston. Miss Smyth has meticulously dusted the tea table for us." Moose came in and bowed over her hand with such grace, she blinked in awed appreciation. Yet she didn't miss the veiled look he threw Ford. "I am so very pleased to see you again. I called at the Winter Palace but they informed me you had checked out."

"She's on the Emerald Empress with me, Moose," Ford interrupted. His quick upward glance at the lieutenant was an unmistakable signal.

She'd been right not to confide everything in the handsome policeman, who probably would have reported it all to his old friend, Ford. She'd been so close upstairs; so close to finally getting to the truth. Now she wasn't quite sure of Ford's intentions.

The square table was already set with an old embroidered cloth, three teacups, two matching pots and the other necessary accoutrements. The tea was Earl Grey, her favorite, and the liquid felt refreshing after their trek through town, so she finished an entire cup. In that time, Ford gulped down two. Moose, she noticed, drank nothing, only sat back, seemingly relaxed in his chair in a curiously graceful pose. But his dark eyes were sharp, studying her and then Ford. "So tell me, what did you discover on your cruise to Dendera?"

His voice was surprisingly soft and lyrical for such a large man, or was that part of the deception, too?

"We haven't found out where Charlie has gone off to," Ford growled, pouring himself yet another cup of tea. The room itself seemed to be hushed and waiting, like a summer day before a storm.

"Don't you think it's time the authorities became involved in the search? Or do you have a plan of your own, Ford?"

The question shattered the atmosphere into a million fragments tense with anticipation. For a second, she couldn't breathe, she could only focus on the blue of Ford's eyes blazing in his tanned face. Wouldn't he tell his friend his plan—that is, if it was legal—or would her presence stop him? She knew the lieutenant was there, watching them, but for one moment the room held only the two of them. She stared straight into Ford's face, looking for answers.

A loud cough from the open door broke the spell. Miss Smyth again! The woman had a dreadful sense of timing. She stood rigidly at attention, obviously disapproving. "The second under secretary of the Antiquities Ministry is here to see you, Dr. Harris. And Miss Zacharias has also arrived looking for Miss Cranston."

"Why would Akim be here?" Ford asked, looking pointedly at Moose.

"He called and requested a meeting with both of us." Moose rose to greet the under secretary as he entered the room, though when Farita walked in after him, he seemed distracted for just a moment.

Farita was full of concern, Olivia noted. Why did the woman think Olivia had to explain her movements to anyone? Perversely, she sat sipping her tea as if she was perfectly at ease.

"Miss Cranston, how pleasant to see you once again." Akim's bow didn't even come close to Moose's earlier perfection. "Your guide and I arrived at the same moment. I fear she means to take you away."

Farita glanced uncertainly between Olivia and the official. "I apologize for the interruption, but Mr. Mujod has requested the tour members meet earlier than announced for a presentation on Karnak by one of the local guides before we visit there tonight." She smiled brightly at Ford. "You, sir, are not required. I had been out searching the bazaar and Lois told me I might find Olivia here."

The guide pointedly avoided the lieutenant's gaze. She didn't look at him or even acknowledge he was in the room. When Olivia turned toward Farita, the guide seemed almost flustered, which was odd. Olivia had found her to be amazingly self-confident for a woman in this male-dominated society.

"I was certain you would not wish to miss it."

"Good idea, Farita," Ford said.

Olivia swung around to Ford in protest. She wanted to deal with Charlie's disappearance, Ford's lies—everything—right this minute!

"You should stay with your tour group this afternoon. Then tonight, I'll meet you at Karnak for the show."

She stared at the silent circle of men, understanding that nothing she could say or do would break through the determination she saw on Ford's face.

"All right," she capitulated, not liking it one bit. "Good day, gentlemen."

Moose surged toward the door, tripped on the edge of the worn oriental rug and stumbled, just managing to catch himself on the door frame to keep from falling. Closest to him, Farita paused to stare for a second in surprise, but didn't say anything. As he bowed them out, the young woman turned away in apparent confusion.

Olivia could feel Ford's eyes on her. Looking around, she sent a determined glare to tangle with his. *Tonight,* she promised him silently. Tonight she wouldn't back down until all the cards were on the table, faceup.

"About my letters to Charlie?" She couldn't think of any other way to refer to the notes he still had. She really didn't want to leave them with Ford.

"Don't worry," he said. "I'll bring them to you tonight."

Tonight, she fumed all the way out into the courtyard. Tonight she'd put an end to his game playing one way or another!

"ARE YOU ALL RIGHT, Moose?" Ford asked, astonished at his friend's uncharacteristic clumsiness.

"The frayed edges of this carpet are treacherous."

Watching him walk back to the table with his accustomed grace, Ford shrugged. He needed to finish this business now so he could concentrate on reading through Charlie's astonishing notes.

All of the artifacts Charlie mentioned were instrumental in the lore surrounding the cult of Osiris. This convinced Ford that Charlie couldn't possibly be actively working with the cult, or have stolen the tablet from the Book of the Dead. Charlie had his faults—he could definitely be overzealous in his work—but the man wasn't stupid. Would he have left such copious notes if they could connect him to something illicit?

No, he wouldn't have. But then, Charlie must have known his research was putting him in danger from those who had less scientific purposes for the articles he hunted.

And now they had him...

Something in these papers would lead him in the right direction. And once he got Olivia out of harm's way, he could go after the young man without hesitation.

"Sit down, Akim." Ford felt he had to be gracious. "I'll have Miss Smyth serve us more tea. Exactly what brings you to Luxor?"

"I fear I have no time for pleasantries." He looked nearly as strained as he had at the time of his wife and son's deaths. "The ministry has sent me to inspect any damage caused by the earthquake."

Ford motioned the man to a chair and sat when Akim did. Moose chose to stand at the desk and folded his arms across his chest.

"I have been sent to confer with the engineers who are inspecting all the temple sites between here and Aswân." His voice sounded so dejected, Ford knew there must be more. "Also, I have been ordered to meet with Interpol agents about recent thefts of Egyptian treasures in Europe. However..."

"What? When is the agent to contact you?" Moose's face turned five shades of angry red.

Confusion was the last expression Ford expected to see on Akim's masculine features. "All I have been told is that I will be contacted when they wish my assistance. They may wish to question members of the Institute staff again about our own thefts, Ford. Until then, it appears we will both be passengers on the Emerald Empress."

"Why wouldn't Interpol come to me first?" Moose persisted.

"My sentiments precisely, Lieutenant. However, I have my duty to perform." Akim sighed, spreading his hands in the Egyptian gesture of resignation.

Suddenly, Ford was fed up. Interpol had told him the same thing. Sit tight. Carry out all ransom instructions until we make contact. Charlie was missing! The damn cult *and* Interpol were pulling his strings as though he were a puppet. It had gone on long enough!

Realizing that both men were waiting for his reaction, Ford stood. "We're not solving any of our problems by sitting around here."

"I agree." Akim recovered enough of his poise to stand and smile. "I believe I will start by meeting the engineers at Karnak."

"I'll go with you," Ford said, pleased that would work into his plans to meet Olivia there tonight. By then, he would have figured out what to do with her. A hot coil unwound in his gut. She might be messing up his plans left and right but there was something about her that made him think of an old-fashioned word—one he refused to think, much less say.

"Meanwhile, keep an eye on Olivia, Moose." He shot his friend a long steady look.

"Miss Cranston is in some kind of danger?" Akim's smile faded. "What has occurred?"

"Nothing."

Moose's face said more than his words ever could. He knew Ford was keeping his own counsel. "Do you have something you want to tell me?" he asked softly.

Ford felt guilty. He knew he could trust Moose, but he couldn't trust them, the unknown members of the cult. They might have penetrated into the least likely places, so he had to be careful. "Just help me keep her out of trouble until I figure out a way to get her to go back to Cairo. She shouldn't be here, poking around, getting into who knows what kind of trouble. We don't need another Cranston lost."

It was good to finally be taking charge. To hell with Interpol! Now that he had Charlie's papers, he'd follow the trail himself!

ONLY A FEW TOURISTS wandered on the short approach to Karnak's first pylon later that day. The earthquake must be keeping visitors away, Ford thought. The delicate balance of Egypt's economy, entirely dependent on the world's interest in archaeological sites, would be in deep trouble if tourism declined.

Three engineers were in the first courtyard, already inspecting the wide columns that had at one time supported a cedar roof. There was no grander place in all of Egypt, nothing that stood for the engineering knowhow of the ancients like this Hypostyle Hall. Ford looked up. If one of these stone giants had been disturbed, if it should topple, everything around and beneath it would be destroyed.

Leaving Akim to confer with the engineers, Ford moved through the third pylon, anxious to inspect the obelisks. He hadn't been here for six months, but

Tuthmosis I's solid pink granite obelisks were his personal favorites. They were one hundred and forty-three tons each and one had already fallen during the eighteenth century. The other was leaning slightly and a constant concern. He spent an hour going over this treasure, remeasuring its angle, testing the soil and granite surrounding it. By the time he was finished, he could certify it was still safe, but the blazing sun had turned his shirt to a sweat-soaked rag that clung to his skin.

Akim brought the engineers to find him, and together they moved slowly through the enormous complex. They tagged the two statues of Ramses III that framed his temple entrance, and the portico at the small temple of Tuthmosis III for further inspection.

The relentless heat finally caused Akim to put aside his dignity and remove his coat and tie. Rivulets of perspiration ran from under Ford's hat and down his face. The clear water of the quadrangular sacred lake looked so damned tempting, he thought he might forget custom and offend everyone by plunging in to cool off. Instead, he unbuttoned his shirt all the way, letting any small breeze cool his chest as the sun began to drop in the sky.

Akim smiled. "I think we have accomplished quite a bit today. And at least the engineers know the proper procedure now to continue their inspections."

Ford glanced at his watch. "It's good we found so little damage. I must be going, I promised to meet Olivia."

"It is regrettable that she should arrive to visit her brother when all is in such a state of unrest. What do you plan to do about all these...difficulties?" An expression of avid curiosity lit Akim's eyes.

"First, I'm going to find Charlie for her. Then I'll deal with the Interpol problem. Right now, I feel like I'm running out of time."

"Although I appreciate your eagerness to see such a woman, don't you think it would be wise to change first?" Too polite to mention Ford's sweat-and-dirt-stained clothing directly, Akim bowed in farewell.

Checking his watch one last time, Ford made a decision. If he ran to Institute House and bypassed Miss Smyth by using the side door, then took a cab back, he would make Karnak just as the tour started.

ALL AFTERNOON, Olivia had been trapped in the lounge, wedged on the love seat between Irmentrude and Lois. Even Marta had done her part in pinning her in by pulling a chair so close that Olivia would have had to knock her over to get up. Half the occupants in the room were dozing. Between the English- speaking guide's presentation and the French and Italian interpreters, it all seemed endless. Ray sat at the bar like the Sphinx, staring straight ahead, lost in a world of his own. Han was sound asleep in one corner, but his wife was listening diligently, even taking notes.

Olivia glanced around for a chance at liberation and found Stephen lounging next to the door, sending cheeky grins toward Marta at every opportunity.

She murmured something polite and struggled to get up, desperate to find Ford. Irmentrude reached over and patted her arm.

"The lecture's just about done, dear. Mustn't be rude to the fellow."

Resigned, Olivia slid back down. Where was Ford? And, more important, what was he up to? She had hated to leave her brother's notes and would have liked to be going over them herself right this minute. She really had no reason to trust Ford; yet, he'd said he would meet her at Karnak for the night tour. Maybe she was being naive, but she believed him.

The instant the long-winded speech on Karnak ended, she surged to her feet.

"Oh, my, that was so informative, wasn't it?" Lois said, yawning.

"Yes. Please excuse me." Olivia stepped past her.

Somehow, Irmentrude blocked her way. "Miss Cranston, Stephen and I would enjoy your company during our tour of Karnak this evening."

Olivia perceived that her being alone in Egypt upset the English matron's notion of propriety and smiled sweetly at the older woman. "Thank you, but don't worry about me. Dr. Harris is meeting me there."

"Dr. Harris?" Marta appeared at Irmentrude's side, blocking Olivia's escape completely. "He is such an interesting man. I would enjoy knowing him better. Is yours a private tour or can others join in?"

The knowing look in the younger woman's eyes sent hot jealousy rushing into Olivia's chest. Horrified by her own reaction, she forced a laugh. "I'm sure Dr. Harris would be delighted to show you around Karnak."

"Yes, I'm sure he would. I hope you don't mind if I join you?"

Her purr of self-satisfaction opened Olivia's eyes to a whole new view of Marta, and she took a strong dislike to what she saw. "Of course I don't mind. Now if you'll excuse me..."

She pushed past the women and hurried toward the stairs, feeling as if her fellow passengers were entirely too concerned about her. She hadn't gotten very far when Freya and Han confronted her. "Have you seen our daughter?" Freya asked.

The question was totally unnecessary, as Marta was clearly in view. Were all these people deliberately trying to keep her from Ford?

She looked into the woman's cold blue eyes and replied rather sharply, "She's right there talking with Irmentrude and Lois."

She waded through the animated members of the French tour, nodding and smiling and pretending complete ignorance of their language. Finally, she made it to the top of the stairs and ran down to the first landing, where Ray stopped her.

"Um, Olivia, hi." He smiled apologetically, seeming very ill at ease. "Have you seen Dr. Harris? I, um, have a question to ask him about Karnak."

Stunned to think anyone could have any questions after the lengthy ordeal they had just been through, Olivia shook her head. "He'll be at the temple tonight if you want to talk to him."

"Oh, uh, good." He rammed his hands into the pockets of his expensive trousers. "Where are you going in such a hurry? I don't think it's time for us to board the van yet."

"I've got to run to my room for a few things. Please excuse me!"

He lifted graying eyebrows at her tone, but finally allowed her to pass. She made the second staircase with no problem and turned the corner into the corridor for her cabin. Up ahead, by her door, Stephen stood. For one heartbeat, she thought he was coming out of her room.

"Stephen?"

He took a staggering step toward her and she noticed a silver flask in his right hand. When he spotted her, he whipped it into his pocket, flushing to his eyebrows.

"Hello, Miss Cranston. My Aunt Irmie with you?" He looked over her shoulder like a frightened little boy.

"No, she's still in the lounge." She eyed him warily as she slid past to her door. "We're leaving soon for Karnak."

There could be no mistaking his pained expression. "Lecture gave me a bit of a thirst." Grinning his Cheshire-cat smile, he straightened and slicked back his hair with his palms. "Be seeing you."

Although he tried to walk in a straight line, he couldn't quite make it. Olivia feared for one of the antique sconces in the corridor when he bumped it as he rounded the corner.

She snapped on her cabin light and sat down on the side of the bed. The travel clock on the dresser was exactly where she'd placed it. Her perfume bottle and makeup were precisely placed by the mirror on the desk. Everything was in order. She must be getting paranoid. Still, she inspected the tiny bathroom and opened her closet door. Everything appeared to be just as she'd left it this morning.

Suddenly remembering Charlie's letters, she opened the desk drawer to lift them out. A sharp stab of fear doubled her over and she sat down hard on the desk chair to take a deep ragged breath. The ribbon wasn't tied correctly. She did her bows with a triple, not a double loop.

Someone *had* been in her room and searched it. And all those nice fellow travelers had been conspiring to keep her upstairs. Anger and fright brought her to her feet. She placed the letters back and slammed the drawer shut. Whipping around, she surveyed the quiet room. Who had done this? Stephen? But why?

A soft rap at her door made her suddenly tense.

"Olivia, it is time to go now." Farita's soft voice came through the paneling.

Yes, she'd go to Karnak and find Ford...she didn't trust him, either, but at least she knew the face of that enemy.

Once on the van, she paused to inspect each and every face. Marta stared at her from her place beside Stephen, who had his eyes closed. Was it the liquor, or was that just a cover? Irmentrude was turned talking with Patty, so Olivia took the opportunity to escape her diligence and slipped into the empty seat behind the driver. Everyone seemed perfectly normal, but she knew they were not. Someone was conspiring against her. Someone had searched her room. Someone didn't want her to find her brother.

Oh, God! Charlie! What was going on here?

The microphone switched on and Farita spoke softly, "Let us imagine, the sun is turning our Egyptian sky mauve and the Nile reaches upward to her with the same color. They mourn the going of Ra."

Olivia turned to look through the minibus window but didn't see anything. For once, Farita's soothing tones failed to placate her. She'd made up her mind. Nothing was going to scare her off. No one was going to keep her from learning the truth about Charlie, not her fellow passengers, and especially not Ford.

When she found him, she would make him tell her what he knew. She would confront him about the amulet and then, once and for all, she would know...

What had Charlie gotten himself into? She fought the fear for her brother that made her tremble inside. To help him, she would have to be strong. This wasn't like their childish games when she sensed he was in trouble and ran to his rescue. This was deeper and deadlier; and, for the first time in her life, she didn't know with absolute certainty what she should do.

The bus pulled to a stop in a parking lot filled with similar vehicles. Far to the right, against a black sky sparkling with stars, rose colossal walls of stone turned gold and alabaster by strategically placed floodlights. It was a magnificent sight, but not enough to deter her from looking for Ford.

Unfortunately, he was nowhere to be seen. Perhaps he was waiting inside. She followed her group, plus hundreds of other tourists, all of them converging at the entrance to Karnak. Panic set in like a lead weight in her stomach. How would she ever find him? What if he wasn't here?

At the head of the group, Farita and Mujod stopped momentarily. Olivia felt claustrophobic as the crowd pressed and shifted around her.

"Please, the show will begin at any moment. It shall unfold as we move from here to the open courtyard, on through the Hypostyle Hall, into the heart of the complex, until finally we arrive at the sacred lake."

Mujod cleared his throat and declared rather importantly, "Make sure you have your flashlight in your possession. The way is uneven and at times poorly lighted."

Olivia stuck her hand into her blazer pocket and curled her fingers around the small metal flashlight to reassure herself. Suddenly, all was plunged into darkness as the floodlights vanished to be replaced by a flickering ghostly light playing across the high stone pylons. Symphonic music trumpeted through the sultry still night air.

"May the evening soothe and welcome you, oh weary traveler," a feminine voice enunciated crisply over the loudspeaker system.

"You now enter the fabulous complex that for two thousand years only priests and pharaohs were allowed to enter," intoned a male voice. "Hear the whispered response of the ever-present god. Come, oh visitor, do not be overwhelmed by the sheer size of this holy place. It was not designed for men, but for gods."

Carried by the impetus of the crowd, Olivia found herself in the inner courtyard, a place of piled stones, shadows and hollow pylons with inner stairways leading to the ramparts of heaven. A huge granite statue of Ramses II was at her back, and looming overhead were tall columns blotting out the moon's light.

"All the magnificence of the pharaohs is represented here at Karnak. I am the father of fathers. The mother of mothers. The bull of seven celestial kind." Now voices spoke in unison. "I cause all to be, that men should have a path on which to tread. Come, follow me."

"We will move on. The way is dark. Use your flashlights," Farita urged.

Obediently, Olivia reached into her pocket for her flashlight. She shivered suddenly, though the night was hot and still. Where was Ford? Had he abandoned her? She glanced around, deliberately concentrating on the people closest to her. Farita darted about, trying to keep her charges together. The four friendly ladies from Indiana, their faces glowing with excitement, surrounded her.

Had they searched her room?

"There you are, Olivia! Sorry I'm late!" Ford pushed to her side, his blond hair silver in the moonlight.

Overwhelmed by the relief she felt, she snapped at him, "I've been looking all over for you."

He caught her arms tightly. "What's happened?" His demand was so loud, people around them, including Farita and Mujod, turned to stare.

"Easy, Ford." Only then did she realize that Moose was there, too.

She swallowed before she could answer. "Something has happened. We need to talk. *Now.*"

"Damn it, Olivia. Go back to Cairo and quit interfering!"

"Please, it is time to go now." Farita moved among the group, clearly trying to defuse the moment. "Here are the guides who will lead us now."

A tall, slender Egyptian man grabbed Olivia's arm, pulling her toward the center courtyard.

Ford looked around, startled, as if he suddenly realized there were people around them. "Okay, let's go ahead and get this over with."

He didn't seem to think there was anything strange about the guide, and knowing Ford was nearby, she felt safe enough to follow the man deeper into the complex.

"Please, the show will continue at any moment. It shall unfold as we move through the Hypostyle Hall, into the heart of the complex, until finally we arrive at the sacred lake," the new guide said.

Other groups and guides jostled around them, making it hard to hear. One guide, leading Marta and her parents, stepped between Olivia and Ford. Others poured into the space, separating them further.

Olivia refused to panic. There were hundreds of people all around her. She stood on her toes trying to see Ford's head over the crowd as her guide urged her on.

"No, we must wait!" She tried to dig in her heels, but he refused to stop.

"Please, follow me." He pulled her around a pylon and through a circle littered with fallen stones.

Fear gave her the strength to wrench herself free. Twirling, she raced back toward the crowd and Ford. They must have turned a corner, for she could see nothing of the tremendous group of tourists. The complex was confusing; every opening and every pylon looked the same to her.

When she whirled about, even her guide had disappeared. She ran through the first doorway in front of her.

She couldn't see anyone. The lights, music and voices were moving away from her and she couldn't get to them. This section of Karnak fell back into a shadowy time and place when only the stars lit the ancient stones.

She looked up to get a bearing on a star, or anything, before starting a methodical search for an exit. Every once in a while, she called, "Ford!" but there was no answer.

She wasn't certain how long she had been wandering alone when she became certain someone was watching her. She spun around but there was no one in sight—only darkness and the shadows of the temple ruin. Yet, she'd felt an intense, hostile stare boring into her back.

She remembered the temple at Dendera, where she'd been frightened for no reason. Ford would come, just as he had then.

Wouldn't he?

"DR. HARRIS, we would so like to join your group." Marta's body blocked his view of Olivia. He took a second to look into her pale face.

"Fine. Come on!" He pushed through the crowd toward where he'd last seen Olivia, Moose on his heels.

Fear ripped through his gut. She was gone.

"Is something wrong?" This time, he didn't spare the young girl a glance.

"Come on, Moose. She's disappeared."

He ran through the first courtyard, Moose beside him. They turned the corner after the first pylon and ran headlong into Farita.

"Have you seen Olivia?" Ford barked out the words, furious with himself for letting her get away from him.

She stopped, out of breath, her eyes huge black pools. "Only with you."

Ford turned and began to run in earnest. There was another, lesser known way out of the complex to the north side between the third and fourth pylons. Moose followed, pulling Farita with him.

The place was a maze. Luckily, Ford knew every enclosure, all the halls and chapels. "Head toward the sacred lake. I'll go this way!" He shouted the words over his shoulder as he turned the other way at Tuthmosis's obelisks.

He jumped down, outside the temple halls and heard her voice call his name faintly.

He stopped. "Olivia!"

Her response sent him racing through the open-air museum, filled with the crumbled pieces of Karnak. He vaulted over anything in his way and made a beeline for the north gate.

There she was, standing beneath the entrance to the Temple of Ptah. Just above her, a white billowing robe caught his eyes.

"Olivia!" He bellowed her name, sprinting forward, catapulting into her as an enormous block of stone careened down toward her.

Chapter Six

The block of stone grazed his ankle as it smashed to the ground, causing the earth to shake as if it were in the throes of an aftershock.

Ford suddenly realized he was on top of her, pushing her slender frame into the sand and gravel. "Olivia, are you all right?" Shaking with worry and anger, he rolled over, pulling her on top of him, running his hands over her body to reassure himself she wasn't harmed.

Unable to stop himself, he cupped her face in trembling fingers and kissed her with the fervor of a grateful man who had just missed losing what he most desired. Incredibly, her lips parted at his coaxing and she shifted her body to fit into his like the long-lost piece of a complex puzzle.

In another moment, he'd be lost. He forced himself to pull away from her. Standing, he helped her to her feet. When she saw the size of the stone block, she began to shake and leaned against the pylon to catch her breath.

The assailant would be long gone but Ford made a quick survey of the area, anyway. There was nothing to show him who might have tried to harm her, although he could guess—an overzealous cult member, trying to scare her away. He was just about to climb the rock to check the top of the pylon when Moose arrived, still holding on to Farita's hand.

"Is she unharmed?"

Farita seemed stunned by the turn of events. She took Olivia's hand and patted it in support. Out of nowhere, Mr. Mujod materialized, followed by the rest of the tour members. When they realized what had almost happened, Lois started to scream, the women from Indiana closed around Olivia protectively and everyone else was asking questions.

Mr. Mujod tried desperately to calm the group. "An unfortunate accident. The stone must have loosened during the recent quake. The authorities will be notified. We are so fortunate that no one was injured."

"Everybody can relax. Olivia is fine." Ford's matter-of-fact tone put an end to the babbling. But their shock at her appearance couldn't be contained.

Even though her elegant outfit was ruined, and her hair tangled in a wild mane around her pale oval face, Olivia's eyes were full of determination. "I am perfectly all right—thanks to Dr. Harris."

Mr. Mujod shook his head. "We must report this to the engineers at once."

Ford looked at the block of stone, then at Mujod. They'd been all over the temple this afternoon and had seen nothing to indicate a stone was loose. This was no accident, it was sabotage—aimed at Olivia. But if Mujod wanted to downplay the incident, Ford would go along. No use in worrying Olivia further. He broke into the group of hovering women and put his arm around her.

She glanced at him and then at Farita. "I don't want to spoil everyone else's time here. Please go back. If Dr. Harris will take me to the Emerald Empress, I'll be perfectly fine." Her voice gained strength with each word.

Eager to comply with her demand, he reached out, curling both his arms around her. Shock tightened his gut when she leaned into him. This incident had shaken her more than she wanted anyone to see.

Murmuring and shaking their heads, the tour members moved on. Ford kept his arms around Olivia for support, leading her toward the Avenue of Sphinxes. When they reached the second pylon, she hesitated. Looking up at him, her eyes glistened, catching the intermittent moonlight. "We do need to talk. But I don't want to go back to the ship."

It was impossible for him to respond to the fear he saw in her face. Moose coughed discreetly behind them as Farita, Mr. Mujod and Irmentrude came to look for them.

"I have asked a local guide to escort the tour," Mujod fussed. "My first concern must be Miss Cranston's good health."

"As well it should be!" Irmentrude folded her arms and studied Olivia's face. "I am a midwife at St. Anne's Infirmary in Manchester. In my opinion, Miss Cranston needs a hot bath, a hot toddy and her bed, at once. There will be no badgering her with questions tonight." Her emphatic tone silenced even Mujod.

Olivia's mouth quivered into a meek smile. "That is exactly what I plan to do the minute I get back to the ship. But first... I think Dr. Harris wants to stop by Institute House."

Ford stayed quiet, content to follow Olivia's lead.

"You are an intelligent young woman." The English midwife eyed her critically. "Do you need a physician?"

Olivia shook her head, ebony hair falling across her cheek. "No. I need exactly what you prescribed." She looked at the rest of them. "But thank you all for your concern."

Darting forward, Farita studied Olivia from grave eyes. "It is my fault, Miss Cranston. I should have been more watchful of you. I am so sorry this horrible thing happened to you."

"It's not your fault, Farita. I don't blame you in the slightest."

He'd never heard Olivia's voice sound so sweet, so reassuring. Reaching out, she squeezed one of the young Egyptian guide's hands. Instead of being comforted, Farita burst into tears. Mujod's face twisted into a frown and he whispered something in her ear. Suddenly, she stopped sobbing to bite her full lower lip.

Ford waited for Moose to step in with his usual charm and defuse the situation, but his friend remained perfectly still. What the hell was wrong with Moose? He knew him well enough to know Moose was attracted to the guide. Didn't he feel the need to comfort her?

Ford certainly knew a great need—to protect Olivia. He tried to moderate the pressure of his arm around her, holding her, giving her unspoken support. Whatever she wanted, whatever she needed, he would go along with.

"Olivia, we'll go in Moose's car. Give me your keys, Moose."

"I will drive you," Moose volunteered readily.

"No, please!" Ford felt Olivia's tension all along his body.

Stunned, Moose stopped and stared at her. Ford hadn't expected this. Exactly what was Olivia afraid of? He had to find out. He sent his friend a silent message, hoping he'd understand.

As Moose handed over the car keys, he insisted, "I shall stop by Institute House, later, to check on you, if that is all right."

"Yes. Thank you." Her voice quivered and Ford saw a tear form on her lashes.

From behind them, Irmentrude cleared her throat. She folded her hands over her khaki shirt and glared at Ford with disapproval.

"Miss Cranston needs her rest. If you are staying with her, I must insist that you do nothing to upset her. Nothing, do you understand? And I must insist that you call me if she requires medical assistance. I shall be in cabin eighteen on the second deck." She paused to draw breath. "Do I have your assurance that I'm leaving Miss Cranston in good hands, Dr. Harris?"

"Yes, ma'am. Trust me, there is no one more concerned about Olivia than I am."

OLIVIA'S MIND RACED with possibilities as she sat beside Ford in the cramped car. It seemed to take mere moments to reach the Institute compound. Ford was all consideration, but they had business to tend to, important business that she had let go too long.

She stopped in the entrance hall. "If Charlie's papers are still in your office, I want to go there."

Without protest, Ford led her down the hall and turned on the overhead light in his office. The place was still an incredible mess. She couldn't understand how a scientist could work in such chaos.

He switched on a low lamp that focused a pool of light on the cluttered desk. She sank into the nearest chair when her knees began to shake.

"Here." He laid Charlie's papers on her lap. "I'm going to get us both a drink."

She looked down at Charlie's familiar handwriting, seeing nothing. Reaction to her near-death experience at the temple was beginning to set in. Her hands trembled, and she clasped one over the other for control.

All the information she needed was right here on her lap. If only she could get Ford to help her...to trust her with the truth.

Clutching the papers in her fingers, she stood up when he stalked back in, carrying two glasses and a bottle of Egyptian wine.

He looked agitated as he poured the wine and thrust a glass into her free hand. "Drink it."

She did as he commanded. The sour taste hung at the back of her throat. "It's awful."

"You'll get used to it if you stay in Egypt long enough." He watched her curiously.

She paced the room, nervous. Ford's fair hair was messed up, his clothes rumpled. He had been through the same frightening experience, yet she could sense anger in him as opposed to her confusion. He knew what was going on, and soon she would, too.

Backing to the desk, she placed Charlie's papers in a neat pile and cleared a spot for her glass. Turning to face him, she gripped the edge of the desk behind her for support.

"I saw you steal the thet amulet from the museum."

His eyes glazed a spectacular blue, but there wasn't a glimmer of fear or desperation in them. "Why didn't you turn me in to the authorities?"

"Because I have this horrible feeling it all has something to do with Charlie. I've been following you around because I'm afraid you're the only person in this godforsaken country who can help me find my brother."

Ford was stunned by her revelations, but still reluctant to tell her anything. She could see it in his eyes—those incredible eyes that revealed more than they concealed.

Desperate, she made a final appeal. "I need to know."

"What made you decide to tell me now?" he said.

He was stalling. She released her numbing grip on the desk and took two steps closer to him.

"I think I've gone about all of this the wrong way. I know Charlie. And through him, I know you. You archaeologists are brilliant, honorable and totally committed. If you weren't, half the priceless antiquities gracing museums around the world would have been sold to the highest bidder. Something more is going on here. You're not a thief. And I'm not stupid."

She walked up to him, put her hand on his arm and looked steadily into his face. "This afternoon, someone searched my cabin. That stone at the temple was pushed. Before I get us both killed, don't you think you should tell me what's going on?"

Suddenly, he came to life, pulling her to him, enfolding her in a crushing embrace. At that same instant, she heard a door open and shut in the distance. She went rigid.

"It's only Moose. Why didn't you want him to come with us earlier if you knew you were going to confront me with my theft?"

As they stared into each other's eyes, she felt a catch in her throat. "I know he's your friend, but I was afraid he might feel a moral obligation to turn you in if he knows about your taking the amulet. I don't want that."

She saw his astonishment, then his body seemed to relax in a sigh. Before she could stop him, he kissed her in the same intimate way he had at Karnak. He lifted her off her feet and swung her gently into a chair.

"Sit. It will be okay now. We're going to talk this through."

Excitement, a feeling of being swept up and into a combustible mixture of danger and desire, kept her rooted to the spot.

At that moment, Moose walked into the room. Ford handed him his own untouched glass of wine. "Here, you'd better sit down. We've got a lot of planning to do."

The nostrils of Moose's thin aristocratic nose flared and his dark eyes glowed with anger. "It is about time we planned together, Ford." He looked pointedly at her. "Charlie's continued absence would indicate he cannot return. If someone *is* holding him against his will, why? What do they want from him? I believe you can tell us." The last he directed at Ford.

"Damn! I'm sorry to get you both messed up in this." Now it was Ford's turn to pace the faded carpet. "I just can't come up with any other way to keep Olivia safe until we figure this out."

That ache expanded upward into her chest. "My brother's disappearance has something to do with his search for the hand of Osiris, doesn't it?"

Before Ford could answer, Moose sucked in a deep breath and leaned forward. "My men have confirmed that several of the small villages between Luxor and Aswân have become involved in this new Osiris cult."

Cult? A shiver ran through her body. Ford kneeled on the floor beside her and reached for her hand, holding it in a tight grip.

"That doesn't necessarily mean Charlie has become involved in any of this . . . this . . . What does an Osirian cult do, anyway?" she asked. The look that passed between the two men froze her blood.

"They have him, Olivia. You were right about the amulet. I stole it to exchange for Charlie's freedom. That was the price they demanded."

Maybe it was the late hour, or the fact she'd narrowly escaped death; whatever the reason, her mind couldn't grasp the meaning of his words. She could only shake her head, staring at him.

He grabbed her other hand and leaned closer. "Because of Charlie's notes, I now know they need the amulet for their ceremony. These cultists believe that they can be resurrected like Osiris, provided what was done for him by the gods is done for them. They make use of amulets and magical texts of all kind, and perform ceremonies in order to compel Isis to act on their behalf."

Fear chilled Olivia's blood. "Stop beating around the bush and get to the point!" At her desperate whisper, Moose stiffened and glanced at Ford.

"Look at me, Olivia," he said firmly.

She felt his warm breath fan the side of her neck like a caress, but there was a hard edge in his voice. Shocked and frightened, she shifted to face him.

"During the ceremony, the rich sacrificed oxen and deer, poorer folk sacrificed geese and guinea fowl. The animals were then wrapped in bandages of linen before they were burned in the god's honor. Fanatical fringe elements were rumored to use—"

"No!" Her upward lunge toppled the chair backward. "Even I know the ancient Egyptians never used human sacrifices." She stood staring at Ford, willing him to confess he had been pulling some stupid, cruel gag at her expense.

"Look, Olivia, I'm not saying Charlie is going to end up wrapped like a mummy and sacrificed for a village's immortality. I'm telling you he's got himself involved in a mess. From his notes, I now realize this cult is gathering all the talismans for the ceremony. Someone, not me, stole the tablet containing the resurrection passage from the Book of the Dead last month from the museum. My guess is that the rash of robberies in Europe of Egyptian antiquities can be laid at the cult's door."

Terror exploded inside her. "What can we do? Why didn't you notify the authorities immediately?"

"I did. I called Interpol." He straightened her chair and made her sit down again. "They told me to do whatever the cult asked. I'm sure they have me under surveillance."

The same powerful jolt of electricity she felt every time he touched her started her trembling again. "Is that why you booked passage on the Emerald Empress?"

"Yes. I was to carry the amulet at all times. I would be notified when and where the exchange would take place. Except now, I think the cultists have something else in mind. Remember the intruder at the Winter Palace?"

Remember! She'd been guilt-ridden ever since for feeling this astonishing pull of attraction for Ford when Charlie was in danger. Her throat tightened with tears, so she just nodded.

"Has anything else occurred, Ford?" Moose shot the question at him.

"I got a message that night at the hotel to go to the Osiris Chamber at Dendera, but I think Olivia scared off my contact. Then, when I got back to the ship, there was another message on my bed—the symbol for Horus at Edfu."

Olivia gasped in horror. Had her own actions prevented her brother's release?

Ford's eyes clashed with Moose's. "I know. That means not only is Interpol on board with me, so is one, if not more, of the cult members."

Olivia was shaking deep inside, appalled at the thought that her headstrong pursuit of Ford was endangering her brother. She withdrew into her own thoughts, brooding while the two men speculated about their next course of action.

"There appears to be only one thing to do. I will sail on board the Emerald Empress with you," Moose said.

"You and I may have to get back aboard the Emerald Empress, but Olivia sure as hell doesn't. Someone's already searched her cabin. And the incident tonight at Karnak was no accident. It was a warning to stay out of the way. I won't put her in any more danger!"

She must be going crazy! As she regained her equilibrium, the coolly rational part of her reappeared. She had never been so terrified in her whole life, yet she felt so gloriously alive. There was serious work to be done now. She turned to the desk and swept up Charlie's notes.

"Short of throwing me in Moose's jail, you can't stop me from going back on board the ship. We have Charlie's papers. Why can't we use them to find him? I don't imagine you like having some sick cult, or even Interpol, telling you what to do any more than I do." She handed Ford her brother's legacy. "If you don't know who's who on board ship, it makes sense for there to be two of us to watch your back."

Electricity flashed between them, making her feel hot and powerless. A pulse beat so loudly in her ears, she could hardly hear what he murmured in a low husky voice.

"I'd tell you to go back to Cairo and wait for me until this mess is cleared up, but I know you won't."

Instead of answering, Olivia just studied him until his mouth softened. She took a long deep breath, and at the same time Moose gave one short discreet cough.

"Now that we have decided our course of action, I suggest we board the ship. It sails at midnight for Edfu."

Suddenly, Ford looked totally different. Gone was the openness, the sharing. The analytical scientist had returned.

Sifting through the papers, he ran one hand through his tousled hair. "According to this, Charlie found some clue at Edfu that led him to the location of the Osiris box. That's when the cult must have taken him. I'd bet they were following him for months." He gave her one more long look before his mouth curled in a dazzling smile, at once intimate and daring. "If you're ready, we're off to Edfu to pick up your brother's trail."

THE EMERALD EMPRESS was quiet when they trooped into the reception area at three in the morning. A sleepy guard checked their boarding passes, and was so impressed when Moose flashed his badge, he saluted.

Ford followed Olivia into her cabin and shut the door behind him. Moose had quietly slipped away, leaving them alone.

"I'll check out the place for you. Then you'd better go to bed. Irmentrude is right. You need your rest for what's ahead of us."

Totally exhausted, she watched him look around her tiny bathroom, then open her closet doors. She felt as if he was her tender protector and she reveled in the care he was taking with her. At no other time in her life had she ever considered doing what she was about to do.

She'd known scores of handsome, smart men, but she hadn't trusted them the way she trusted this man. She hadn't burned inside when they kissed her. Right now, she needed, wanted, what only Ford could give her.

While he looked under her bed, she kicked off her shoes and shrugged out of her jacket.

"If you're afraid to leave me alone, I have a suggestion," she said softly. He looked up, his eyes blazing, and she backed away one step. Her heart banging against her ribs, she smiled slowly. "Stay with me tonight."

He uncurled, rising to his full height, staring at her with such intensity his eyes darkened fiercely. "You know I want you, Olivia. I made that plain from the beginning. If I sleep in this bed, there's no way we won't make love. Is that what you want?"

With his blond hair falling into his eyes, he looked boyish and vulnerable. A wave of heat washed over her, making it hard to breathe.

"I don't want promises or words neither of us mean." She kissed him, pressing against him, wanting him, needing him to want her just as badly. "But, I don't want to be alone tonight. No strings attached for either one of us."

He went as still as one of the statues she'd seen at Karnak. Even in shadow, his eyes still blazed. She could sense his struggle, and knew the moment he capitulated.

Heat danced under her skin as he slid his fingers into her hair and kissed her with slow, open-mouth, moist kisses that went on and on until she was limp with longing. He eased her into the bed, their bodies tangled together, hot and tight.

She had to be out of her head, for what she felt at this moment as he kissed her with such exquisite tenderness was more stirring than anything she'd ever known. His hands brushed her shirt aside, her breasts tingled at his touch. Breathless from pleasure, she became light-headed as he caressed her into nakedness.

She kept her eyes closed, afraid to look at him. Afraid he'd see what she felt. No complications. That's what she'd said. That's what she wanted.

But she couldn't deny her sensual side, couldn't keep still when he pressed kisses across her aching breasts. Her legs came up to wrap around his body, to hold him to her. His lips were so light, so teasing, she gasped and buried her face in his hair, loving the sun-scorched smell of it.

Under the veil of her closed lids, lights sparkled. Her breath came faster between her parted lips. She felt herself soar at his touch, a thousand colors and designs colliding in her mind.

He kept kissing her, the length of her body, down her shins to her instep. For a moment, she lost all touch with reality. Then she knew he was naked, his flesh hot and moist pressing against her.

"Open your eyes and look at me." His whisper broke into the swirling darkness around her.

His eyes gauged her reaction as they came together. His face altered, its unearthly beauty sharpening while her body shuddered over and over around him. The heat, the exquisite sensations exploding inside her, bursting from him, broke free everything she kept secret. She flung back her head, unable to speak, only to feel.

Hours, or perhaps mere minutes, later he curled around her and lay still, his breath sweet on her shoulder. Olivia knew he was falling asleep. He breathed deeply, one hand still caressing her breast.

"I love you, Olivia."

It was a sleepy voice, out of a dream, she told herself. Even though she knew he wouldn't hear her, she felt she must answer.

"Don't say that." Tears burned her eyes and blurred her voice. She was glad he couldn't see her.

Suddenly, she felt the bed shift beneath her and a picture rattled in its frame on the wall.

"The earth moved!" she whispered, startled.

"I know, love. But this time it's an aftershock. We'll have them for weeks," was his sleepy reply.

Then came silence and the soft sound of his low, even breathing. Without disturbing him, she eased out from under his embrace and slipped off the bed. She found her silk robe in the closet and went to the window to stare out at the moonlight reflected on the Nile.

The boat started to move, upriver to Edfu.

Ford was outrageously sensual, she rationalized. That had to be the only reason for those flashes, those long moments when there had only been the two of them, nothing and no one else in the whole world. She'd never known that before.

She shut her eyes, trying not to think about what had just happened with Ford. She wanted to empty her mind of danger, desire, everything, for just this one peaceful moment before she had to face what lay ahead.

Suddenly, terror knifed through her. She gasped and her eyelids snapped open, although she saw nothing. Charlie called to her, needing her. Squeezing her eyelids shut again, she tried to send him a message that she was nearby.

Guilt doubled her over in pain. Sagging against the window, she let her tears run down the glass. She'd let desire blot out her only reason for being here: Charlie. She needed to be strong, now more than ever before in their lives.

ROLLING OVER in the bed, Ford reached for Olivia's sweet soft warmth. She was gone!

His eyes snapped open as he sat bolt upright. His heartbeat turned to normal when he saw her standing at the window. Silently, he moved toward her, needing to touch her. Just as he'd known from the beginning, their lovemaking had proved he would always need to be with her, to love her. It struck him as ironic that out of this mess, which threatened to destroy his career and a good friend, he had found the one person he needed in his life.

"Olivia, love, what's wrong?"

She turned, looking at him through a film of tears. "Please don't call me that. I've made a terrible mistake." Tears slid down her face and her voice quivered.

"It was not a mistake," he protested, fear pooling in his gut.

She held up her hand for silence. "Charlie is in grave danger and we're the only ones who can help him. We have to concentrate on that. Nothing else!"

Afraid to ask any more questions, afraid to hear the answers, he took her unyielding body into his arms. After that first vulnerable moment, Olivia shut down her emotions, her eyes dried up and her face paled in the moonlight. Her controlled withdrawal aroused all his protective instincts.

Trying to be gentle, repressing the tidal wave of his need to crush her to his naked body, to coax her into taking back her words, he pulled her down onto the chair in front of the window. He held her while she drifted off to sleep, exhausted.

Ford held her all through the night, then watched dawn break over Edfu.

Chapter Seven

Olivia woke suddenly, the scent of Ford clinging to her skin, her hair, the pillow she pressed to her face.

Her body softened in remembrance of Ford touching her, kissing her, loving her. And, following the devastating revelation of her brother's need, he had simply held her. Even after she had blurted out her guilt, he had been so undemanding, so comforting.

For the first time in her life, she didn't know how to help her brother. Or herself. The well-organized and tightly controlled threads she had carefully woven into a productive and rewarding life were fraying and snapping all around her.

Ford was gone; she sensed that. At once relieved and disappointed, she stretched, rose and crossed to the window. On the shore, squat reddish-brown buildings were an ugly contrast to the brilliant blue sky. The town was busy. On the narrow streets, donkey carts vied with cars, and women carried provisions balanced on their heads or supervised small children. Shopkeepers busily hawked their wares, waving their arms in an exaggerated manner to attract as much attention as possible.

Even from here, she could see one of them had tempted Lois and Ray, who were contemplating a length of Egyptian cotton. She rushed to get dressed and join them. Surely the tour would soon leave for Edfu. Could Ford already be there?

As she finished dressing, she heard voices arguing in the hall. It seemed Moose and Irmentrude were having quite a discussion about her welfare.

"Miss Phipps, I am here merely to—"

Olivia pulled her door open with considerable force, causing Moose to lift his thick black eyebrows in surprise. When he saw her, he gave a polite smile. "Ah, here she is now. Good morning, Olivia. Miss Phipps has been inquiring about you."

At Olivia's appearance, Irmentrude's stiff disapproval vanished, replaced by her normal good-humored smile. "I wanted to reassure myself of your well-being. I felt I had been remiss in not insisting on staying with you last night, in case you needed assistance." Irmentrude's round cheeks took on the hue of polished apples. "However, I can see all is well that ends well. I'll save you a place on the minibus. We leave for Edfu in ten minutes. I assume the lieutenant will be accompanying you as a protector."

Without waiting for an answer, she turned on her heel and left. Moose had the grace to look slightly chagrined.

"Are you supposed to be my bodyguard? And where might Ford be?" She forced a cheery note into her voice, determined that no one should realize what had happened between them last night.

His bow couldn't have been more graceful. "As you so wisely surmised, I am indeed guarding you until we meet Ford at Edfu. He said he would go ahead of the group to try to forestall any interference.''

Olivia nodded. ''Let's go, then. I don't want to keep everyone waiting.''

At the end of the gangway, Farita was wringing her hands in concern. Everyone else was already on board the bus. When she saw Olivia, the guide burst into a smile to rival the sun's brilliance. Moose stopped short in front of her, quickly gripping the handrail for balance.

Farita dashed toward them. ''I was just coming to check on you when Miss Phipps assured me you would be along shortly. And here you are!''

Her breathy laughter seemed odd to Olivia. She took Farita's hand. It felt cold, even in this heat. ''I'm quite well now,'' Olivia reassured her. ''You needn't concern yourself with me.''

Farita sucked in a long breath. ''You look well. I am certain all the unfortunate times are behind you.''

''Thank you. I promise I'll try not to be any more bother.''

''And I am here to keep Miss Cranston safe.'' Moose seemed awkward, and his words came out in a challenge rather than a reassurance. Then he clammed up, appearing unpolished and clumsy as he ushered them both into the bus.

The tour members greeted Olivia warmly. Thankful that they refrained from asking questions, she settled down beside Irmentrude, who pointedly shifted her pith helmet from the seat next to her to her lap. Behind her, Stephen looked positively smug; Marta, wearing huge dark sunglasses, sat beside him. His aunt's solicitous concern for Olivia had apparently been a boon to his love life.

Or had it? Suddenly, Olivia remembered that any one of these people could be a cult member. Which of these people were who they seemed?

"I hope Dr. Harris will be meeting us at the temple. He makes it all so fascinating, doesn't he?"

Irmentrude's casual remark hit close to home. A flash of Ford bending over her created a warmth within her—at this moment, she could taste his kiss, smell his suntanned skin, feel his hands caress her. Olivia stared straight ahead, stunned at the intensity of the images rushing through her mind.

"Yes. I'm sure he'll be waiting for us." Trying to cover her reaction, she stared out the window.

Somehow, her purpose was dissolving in emotion. This wasn't like her at all. She had made one terrible mistake. She couldn't risk another. All she could do at this point was to hope that somehow she and Ford would find her brother. Charlie had been at Edfu, he might even be here now, waiting to be traded for the amulet.

She focused on that thought as the bus pulled into a sand parking lot in front of a completely walled temple. She looked around, searching for anything that might be hiding her brother, but there were no other buses or trucks, not even a donkey cart. There was a stone structure outside the pylon, which she assumed was a guardhouse of some kind.

Ford stood at the pylon's entryway. "Welcome to the great Temple of Horus, although little remains of the once-important Edfu of ancient times." He looked directly at her, holding her gaze for the span of several heartbeats, signaling that he had found something.

She held her breath, terrified. Would it lead them to Charlie? Finally, he looked away and she could breathe again.

"Enter." He swept his hand dramatically forward, inviting the tour into the temple. As they followed him, he continued. "The black granite colossus is the falcon symbol of Horus. Note the far doorway—that is the entrance to the sanctuary of Horus. This temple is particularly significant to the Osiris legend because it is here that Horus finally defeated the evil Set, allowing his father's soul freedom to be resurrected."

Again he threw Olivia a direct glance, his eyes very blue in his tanned face. "Of particular interest are the remains of the birth house facing the pylon. Recorded on the wall are pictures of the life of Horus."

Olivia shivered and looked away. He'd found something in the birth house. She wasn't sure she could wait for him to finish his commentary before he could show her. She began to hang back, turning to look behind her, longing to run to the small stone chamber she'd passed earlier without a second thought.

"We will have time to wander the great ruin of Edfu." Farita's voice gathered her flock tighter around her. "First, Mr. Mujod and I will lead you through the inner Hypostyle Hall. And you must enter the sanctuary, a simple room that held the statue of Horus from earliest times."

Olivia dallied in the court, pretending to take note of the colossus, which was a well-preserved, impressive structure. Cecil B. DeMille himself couldn't have done better. Only Ray and Lois stopped at the falcon to take innumerable pictures of one or the other of them posing beside it. Even Moose defected, bringing up the rear of the group headed by Farita, who disappeared into the shadowy hall.

Ford began to walk toward her, but was stopped by Ray, who asked him to take pictures of both him and his wife as they positioned themselves dramatically in front of the falcon.

There was always someone getting in their way. Olivia tried to appear casual, but could hardly contain her curiosity. Finally, she started back to the gateway without Ford.

When he caught up with her, he took her hand. Saying something quietly to the guards, he pulled her outside the wall and started toward the birth house.

"Has anyone tried to contact you yet?" she gasped, almost running to keep up with him.

When they exited the gate, he stopped. "No. There's a relief in the sanctuary that is almost identical to the one at Dendera. I wasted a lot of time in there waiting. They had plenty of opportunity to contact me, but they didn't." He stared down at her, abruptly changing the subject. "You look tired. I was worried about you last night. I understand that time is crucial now...for all of us."

He ushered her into the birth house. "But, I think I've found something in here."

There was no reference to what lay between them—no hint of the passion they'd shared. He was all business now.

Ford pointed at a wall covered with hieroglyphics and the stone etchings which the Egyptians used to record for all eternity their lives and times, but Olivia couldn't see anything out of the ordinary. Then he removed one of Charlie's pages of notes from his trouser pocket and handed it to her.

The lines around his mouth tightened. "The drawings here represent the divine birth of Horus. But look here." He pointed to markings around the representation of Isis and then to something on the notes she held. "What do you think?"

Using her flashlight, Olivia studied her brother's drawing and the stone etchings side by side. Gradually her artistic eye found a similar pattern.

"See here." Without actually touching the wall, she pointed to a drawing of Isis being carried in a procession. "I'm sure the patterning here is the same as it is on Charlie's page. Does Isis have a special temple that she was carried to? It looks to me as if that's what Charlie was interested in."

"Damn it! If I'd studied Osiris as much as Charlie has I'd know for sure and we'd have this puzzle solved!"

She could tell Ford was tense, worried and in no mood for soothing platitudes. It was amazing how, in such a short time, she could read him so well.

"He could be leading us to Philae. The temple there is dedicated to Isis, but those ruins were moved at the building of the Aswân Dam." Frustration drove him from one side of the birth house to the other.

"Aren't we scheduled for Philae tomorrow? Is there any way to get there this afternoon?" she asked.

At last his face relaxed and he stopped his restless pacing. "Charlie was definitely headed upriver. The best and quickest way to get there is on the Nile, unless you fly from Luxor to Aswân. That isn't an option now."

His hands lifted to her shoulders. "I know you're frightened," he said tenderly. "So am I. But you said it yourself—together we'll find him. Then everything will be fine. You haven't made a mistake, Olivia."

"Ford—"

He placed his fingers against her lips, shaking his head to stop her. "No. Don't say anything now. After we find Charlie, we'll have a great deal to say to each other."

"Dr. Harris, everyone is looking for you, wanting your explanations of the scenes in the outer corridor of the temple." Marta's crisp enunciation startled them both and they sprang apart. Until this moment, Olivia hadn't realized how unquestionably the young woman's diction screamed language school.

She studied her as they walked into the main complex. Marta looked almost cartoon-like with her cotton-candy hair frizzled in the bright sun.

"I offered to look for you because you indicated the birth house held particular interest and I thought I might find you there," the girl said.

Olivia stepped back, trying to blend into the shadows as Ford strode through the Hypostyle Hall and out to the west wall. Sure enough, almost everyone was gathered there. Farita was pointing out scenes of interest to the Indiana ladies, but was clearly waiting for the expert to arrive. Olivia wasn't surprised when Marta's ever-vigilant parents crowded in, followed by Stephen and his aunt. Their closeness, the eager looks on their faces, took on a new meaning for her. At least one of these people was the enemy.

Wanting to put some space between herself and them, Olivia moved toward the entrance, where Moose stood, his arms folded across his chest. Until now, she hadn't realized how big a man Moose actually was.

After a few minutes, Lois joined them. "Fascinating place, Egypt. Isn't it?" She sighed. "And the shopping is marvelous!" She lifted a gold chain and huge gold scarab from around her neck to show Olivia. "The prices are dirt-cheap compared to home. Have you bought anything yet?"

Shopping was the furthest thing from Olivia's mind, yet she tried to make her voice friendly. "I haven't found the time."

"Oh, too bad," Lois clucked sympathetically. "But when we arrive in Aswân tomorrow, you'll have another opportunity. According to the itinerary, we have the whole morning free. I can't decide whether to shop or take a felucca trip across the Nile to visit the Aga Khan's mausoleum." She paused dramatically, then winked. "I guess I'll go shopping even if Ray chooses to sightsee. Oh, here they come."

Ford led the group out. The sunlight reflected in his hair and shadowed his eyes. He looked mysterious and sexy. He looked better than ever.

"My, he does fulfill all one's fantasies about dashing archaeologists, doesn't he?" Lois winked again before dashing after him.

Olivia shook her head. She certainly didn't need any reminders of Ford's potency. On the contrary, she was hurriedly attempting to erect a barrier against him, since that was the only way she could keep her mind focused exclusively on Charlie.

After the tour group moved on, Olivia sat on the steps near the granite falcon. Feeling secure with Moose hovering nearby, she closed her eyes, trying to reach her brother.

The sun beat down on the top of her head, hot and bright, making the darkness behind her closed eyelids explode with color. Images danced before her but they had nothing to do with Charlie! She opened her eyes, disgusted. Blinking several times against the glare, she attempted to arrange the world in its proper order.

Off to one side, against the wall in shadow, Moose still waited. About five feet away, Farita leaned wearily against the same wall, shading her eyes in the bright light. If the young woman would move only two feet closer to Moose, she would be in the shade. Why didn't she? Or, more to the point, why didn't he make room for her?

Was he guarding her or watching Farita?

Feeling as if someone had just doused her with ice-cold water Olivia shivered, realizing Farita might not be what she seemed, either.

Sudden panic made her surge to her feet. Everyone was inside, in the gloom and shadows with Ford. But he had no idea against whom to defend himself. She ran into the shadowy temple, trying not to push everyone aside in her eagerness to reach him.

She found Marta practically hanging on his arm as he explained a cartouche to her mother. The angry look in Marta's cold eyes couldn't be mistaken. Olivia's appearance didn't make her very happy.

She struggled to blend into the group, while trying to eavesdrop on everyone's conversations, to no avail.

Either she made a very bad spy or all these people were the nice bunch of tourists they seemed.

Ford was in the middle of the tour from then on. There was no way a private contact by the cult could be made. Discouraged, Olivia couldn't shake the feeling that somehow she'd messed things up once again.

EVEN AFTER all these years in Egypt, the way night fell over the landscape intrigued Ford. The darkness hid everything: the life-giving Nile feeding the strip of green caressing its banks; every bare, brown hole, gully and ridge of the seemingly endless desert. It all merged into one vast murky shadow.

Charlie could be anywhere out there. Ford had to find him, and fast. Time was running out. For some reason, the cult had decided not to contact him today at Edfu. Now what would they do? To perform their ritual of eternal life, they had to have the thet amulet, and they would have to go through him to get it.

He stood at his cabin window, trying to come up with a single idea about where Charlie might have been heading. Would he have thought to leave clues if he hadn't anticipated trouble? And, if he *had,* why hadn't he come back to the Institute or at least tried to get some help?

Ford felt responsible for the whole mess. He had constantly turned Charlie off to this sort of speculation, believing a "true scientist" never flirted with myth; a scientist dealt with facts—provable, researchable facts. So the kid had probably wanted to prove himself before broaching the subject again. But if Charlie *had* come up with some incredible find, it would be the making of him. As long as Ford could get him out of this alive. And deep in his soul, Ford knew he would have done exactly the same thing as Charlie—pursued his dream, no matter what the cost.

Which is what he had done at Amarna, his second season, when he had defied conventional wisdom and found the picture of Akhenaton and Nefertiti surrounded by their six daughters—now in the museum at Oxford. The picture that had been the foundation of his fascination with the beautiful queen. A fascination unbroken until Ford had sighted Olivia crossing the Cairo Museum toward him.

He had wanted her then; now, his desire was tenfold what it had been before making love with her. Just remembering her petal-soft skin perfumed by some exotic scent brought back pleasure in increasing waves over his body.

But until Charlie was out of danger and this mystery solved, he knew he wouldn't experience her sweet caresses again, her searching kisses, her passion exploding around and through him as she flung her head back, arching into him.

He yanked the curtain closed. Agonizing over it would do him no good. He and Moose needed to do some practical planning.

A soft tap at his door brought him up short. It wouldn't be Olivia, but nonetheless, he threw the door open, hoping.

Akim glanced over Ford's shoulder into the empty cabin, allowing a faint smile to pass over his face. "Forgive me, Ford. After I spied the ever-diligent Lieutenant Bey in the corridor leading to Miss Cranston's room, I hoped you would be alone. I wish to speak with you in private."

"Come in." Ford closed the door and gestured toward the couch, wondering what this was all about. "Sit down, Akim."

"No, no, we cannot linger. The dinner gong will be struck soon. We must keep up appearances." Akim shrugged. "The minister's office in Cairo informed me again today that Interpol will soon be in contact with me. There is one matter I wish to clear up before such an occurrence."

He spread his hands in a calming gesture. "Ford, my friend, does young Dr. Cranston's disappearance and his sister's obvious distress have any bearing on Interpol's investigation? Surely you know there were many rumors when Dr. Cranston and the tablet from the Book of the Dead disappeared at almost the same moment."

Though he'd originally had similar doubts, anger exploded inside Ford. It was a matter of loyalty—to Charlie, and now to Olivia, as well. "Charlie is a scholar! If his wild-goose chase actually netted any Osirian relic, I can assure you it would go through all the proper channels!"

After one startled moment, Akim bowed. "I believe you, my friend. But I had to ask, in an official capacity. Tomorrow I must assess the earthquake damage at Philae. I would like you to accompany me. For the other business with Interpol, we can only be patient and wait for them to reveal themselves."

Patience had never been a virtue Ford put much stock in. All during dinner his lack of it burned like acid through his blood. At his end of the oblong table, the four ladies from Indiana asked him innumerable questions about everyday life in ancient times.

Then Patty began questioning him on his specific research. At any other time, he would have found this inquisitiveness charming. Now he found it suspicious.

In fact, he couldn't help but observe everyone at dinner, looking for a sign, a slipup. He couldn't figure out why the cult hadn't contacted him at Edfu. He'd done everything they'd asked, but now he was beginning to get suspicious.

He had hidden the amulet so there was no way they'd get their hands on it without giving him Charlie first. Again, he glanced at each face in turn. They all seemed so innocent. Besides the cult member, there was most likely an Interpol agent aboard who hadn't made contact, either.

He felt like a mouse trapped in a corner by two hungry cats, both licking their whiskers and waiting. Except, he wasn't alone in the corner. Olivia was there, too.

She sat at the opposite end of the table on his same side, so he couldn't even see her. During after-dinner drinks in the upper lounge, Irmentrude kept her isolated in one corner. He got caught by Marta's mother, Freya, who questioned him again about the Osiris legends. Han stood by, stoic as ever, but listening, his eyes narrowed in concentration.

All of these tourists with their unending questions made him burn with suspicion. Curiosity he could understand, but everyone in this group seemed particularly knowledgeable. And nosy.

Finally, Mujod and Akim rescued him from the South African woman by inviting him to share coffee with them at a small table near the bar. Unable to think of an excuse to get to Olivia, he joined them. At least he would be away from all the questions. Yet, if he didn't know better, he'd suspect the whole group was conspiring to keep him away from her.

Across the room, Moose offered no assistance. He slouched against the wall, his hands rammed into his pockets as he eyed the table where Farita sat with the older American couple and Stephen. Ford made faces at him until he finally strolled over to join that group. Even from this distance, Ford could see how the little Farita blushed. He smiled at his friend's effect on women.

After what seemed an eternity, Olivia rose to her feet, bidding Irmentrude good-night. When she moved, the soft lighting in the lounge shimmered on her cream-colored silk dress as it pulled across her breasts, outlining them. His chair scraped back and made a slight sound as he involuntarily rose to meet her.

She stared at him across the width of the room. By some sort of silent agreement, they planned their exit from the lounge to arrive at the top of the stairs at the same moment. Without saying a word, they descended the steps to her cabin corridor. At her door she stopped, flinging her head back. The gesture brought with it such a powerful memory, he had to suck in oxygen to clear his head.

"You don't have to make any excuse, Olivia. I understand. But I want you to know I'll be right outside your door." He wished he'd been able to keep the raspy edge out of his voice.

Something flared in her eyes before she nodded. "Thank you, but no. Both you and Moose need some rest, too. After all, what can happen while we're sailing?"

"Then, I'll give you an extra key to my room." He pressed it into her palm. "If you need me for any reason, if anything frightens you, come get me." He watched her fingers curl around the key as if it were a talisman. "Sleep well."

"You, too. It looks like tomorrow will be *the* day. If Charlie was at Philae, surely we'll find a clue to his location there." She watched his head nod in silent agreement before she closed her cabin door.

He waited to hear the lock being turned, torn by the apparent ease with which she'd withdrawn from him. Her insistence that they not pursue a relationship while searching for Charlie fired his determination to see this at an end. If only he could think of some way to force the cult's hand.

He turned to find Moose waiting a few doors away.

"Olivia is correct, you know. We must stay alert at all times. Their time is running out and we must be prepared to act if they attempt something."

Ford sighed, suddenly weary to his bones. "We dock in Aswân at eight tomorrow morning. Until then, I'll be walking the decks, hoping for some break."

"I shall go with you."

"No, I should be alone in case they finally decide to make contact."

"Then I shall follow my own lead." Moose turned up the stairs toward the lounge, leaving Ford to climb down to the entry level.

He planned to scour every inch of the vessel, even the crew's quarters, to find what he needed. For an hour he climbed up and down stairs, poking into places he had no business. He even found the galley, where he was summarily ordered out.

Weary, he climbed the outer stairs to reach the top deck. The wicker furniture reflected the moonlight, making tiny pools of white in the inky blackness. He flung himself down in a chair to wait.

All the staff was gone but there was one coffeepot still half-full. Ford poured himself a mug of coffee more for something to do than to actually drink it. It was lukewarm and there was no sugar or cream. The caffeine burned in his stomach, much as thoughts of Olivia burned in his brain.

Above all, he had to protect her. He would never admit it to her, but he was beginning to lose hope for Charlie. He'd done everything he'd been told and the cult had made no effort to contact him. Maybe that meant Charlie was already dead.

How could he face Olivia with that news?

Tomorrow at Philae with Akim would be his last chance to pick up an indication of Charlie's trail. If that failed, he wasn't sure what he'd do...

He dozed off, sat up startled and dozed off again. When he awoke, it was nearing dawn. He went down to Olivia's room and pressed his ear to her door. Silence. At least she was getting a good rest.

Reassured, he headed back up on deck. At about four-thirty, Moose joined him, sliding onto the lounge chair beside him. "I've just checked. All is well."

OLIVIA TOSSED and turned all night, but it wasn't until Ford appeared in her dreams and they turned erotic that she awoke, drenched with perspiration. She turned the light on, got up, rinsed herself off and pulled on her silk robe. She spread Charlie's notes around her, desperately trying to decipher where he wanted her to go, what he wanted her to do. Eventually, sleep claimed her again.

A strong aroma of sweet incense stirred her. The room was dark, filled with dry, stale air. She could see a vast treasure trove at the far wall, but found she couldn't move toward it. Straining, she found her hands and feet were bound.

She panicked, thrashing wildly. When she came fully awake, Charlie's papers were scattered around her. She *was* on the Emerald Empress, dawn light streaking through the crack in the drapes. And her hands and feet were not bound.

That dark, cramped room filled with pungent odors must be where Charlie was being held.

She thought she'd get up and tell Ford and reached for his room key. When a soft knock sounded she automatically checked her wristwatch. Five-thirty.

She stumbled, still a little groggy, to open the door.

"Farita!" Olivia stared at the young guide in surprise. She was holding a tray laden with breakfast food, whose aroma made Olivia's stomach growl.

Farita smiled, but Olivia thought she looked strained.

"We made excellent time on the Nile last night. Soon we will dock in Aswân. Mr. Mujod noticed you did not finish your dinner last evening so he suggested I bring an early breakfast to your cabin."

Olivia stepped back so Farita could enter to place the tray on the dresser. "This is very kind of you and Mr. Mujod."

Glancing around with a nervous little smile, Farita backed into the corridor. "Will you be touring Aswân on your own? Or will you join us at the Aga Khan's mausoleum?"

Olivia shook her head, not knowing what Ford had planned for the day. "I think I'll relax on board this morning."

For some reason, that answer seemed to lighten Farita's spirits. "A very good idea, I think. I will leave you to take your tea now."

After the young guide was gone, Olivia wandered over to the tray. There were her favorite hard crackers and wrapped cheese, and a pot of Earl Grey tea. She hadn't realized anyone noticed her preferences or how little she ate.

The tea was hot and strong and sweet. She was beginning to find tea with the sugar already added a refreshing change. Maybe she had developed a sweet tooth from the lack of anything better to eat.

After filling her cup a second time, she peeked out her window. Fingers of pink sky silhouetted a tiny city ahead. Aswân. She sipped her tea as the city grew larger and closer.

After a while, she sat on the edge of her bed and pushed the teacup onto the tray beside it. She hadn't realized how tired she actually was, probably due to her restless, dream-filled night. She took another deep draft of tea, thinking the caffeine might revive her. Her head felt funny so she lay back against her pillow. For some reason, she began to feel worse. The room started to spin slowly clockwise. A little fissure of panic urged her to get up, and the room started to spin counterclockwise.

She needed Ford! Frantic, she felt in her pocket for his key. She needed to tell him about the dark incense-scented room and Charlie. Fighting her fatigue, she started down the corridor toward the stairs. The hallway shrank and expanded around her like an accordion.

She'd been drugged!

Fighting its effects, she decided she'd ask for help from the first person she saw. Then she remembered she didn't know who she could trust. Only Ford.

Stumbling, her hands feeling the way, she made it to his cabin door. Somehow she fumbled the key into the lock and fell inside. Ford would help her. He would protect her.

Blinking a swirling dark mist from her eyes, she tried to focus on the figure standing in front of Ford's closet door. With recognition came incredible fear.

"You!"

Chapter Eight

Ford was uncomfortable. This had to be the worst bed he'd ever slept on. Then, seemingly right beside him, he heard the shouts of the sailors as another boat pulled up alongside. Suddenly, he realized there was no forward motion of the ship, only a gentle rocking.

He jumped up, confused. Oh, God, he was on deck! And the boat had already docked.

From the looks of things, they'd been here for a while. He stretched, staring at the unfamiliar streets of Aswân. On the opposite bank was a rock face with the small dark openings that marked the tombs of former governors.

Damn! Olivia. Ford sprinted down the stairs two at a time.

Moose's head poked around the corner, his liquid brown eyes studying Ford for a moment. He straightened from his lounging position against the wall. "Relax." He smiled. "I took up my post here not fifteen minutes after we docked. All is well."

Ford raised his eyebrows. "Have you checked on Olivia? Is she all right?"

"It is early. No doubt she's asleep. I did not wish to disturb her."

Moose's reassuring tone made Ford grimace. He was getting neurotic. Of course she was all right. He was overreacting from little sleep and over-worry.

Two men struggled up the gangplank, carrying a large rug rolled into a neat cylinder, a momentary diversion.

"For Mr. Mujod," one of them informed the crewman at the desk in a rough dialect Ford could barely understand.

Ford shook his head at Moose in disgust. From behind him, Mujod came thudding down the stairs, waving his arms and shouting. Ford moved out of his way.

"I told Aslik I would examine the rug when I arrived in Aswân. I did not expect him to send it to the ship, I could have easily looked at it in his shop," he announced to the air. Then, sighing like a man who had done his duty, he glared at the carriers. "Since you are here, bring it to my cabin. I shall take a look at it. However, I make no promises." Shaking his head, he led the burdened men up the stairs to his cabin.

Ford and Moose loitered in the lobby, waiting for Olivia to appear. The French tour left the ship en masse to see the great unfinished obelisk at the granite quarry south of town. They were followed by the Italian contingency on their way to the marketplace for treasures from Nubia. At last, several members of their own tour came into the reception area. A few moments later, Farita arrived. As usual, she avoided Moose and was busily counting heads. Everyone talked at once.

Irmentrude wanted to visit the famous Old Cataract Hotel. "Is the interior really like it looks in the movie? Does it have large fans with wooden paddles, plush red carpeting and antique furniture dating back to colonial days?" the Englishwoman asked excitedly.

Ford decided not to spoil her fun; for while the exterior remained just as it appeared in the film, *Death on the Nile,* based on Agatha Christie's famous mystery novel, the interior no longer had barefoot Nubian servants wearing red fezzes to minister to the guests' every whim.

The Indiana ladies' interests focused on the purely historical—after a felucca ride, they were going to Elephantine Island and from there, on to the mausoleum.

Lois announced fiercely that she was going shopping, no matter what, and got no argument from Ray.

They all sounded like typical tourists. They all looked like typical tourists. But Ford kept watching them, looking for a clue. Which one was Interpol? Which one had left the messages on his bed?

For the tenth time, he glanced down the corridor toward Olivia's room, willing her to appear. Marta, her parents and Stephen trooped down the stairs, anxious to tour the more modern aspects of Aswân, including the huge tower at the bend of the First Cataract.

Still there was no sign of Olivia. Worry sliced through Ford. She didn't eat much, but she never skipped a meal. He started up the stairs to check the dining room but the way became blocked by the two men hauling the rug back down. It had obviously been rerolled in a hurry, for it was lumpy and uneven.

Mujod yapped at their heels. "Tell your employer I am shocked at the inferior workmanship of this piece. I shall no longer be recommending his shop to any of my clients!"

Heads bowed, the men slinked away, down the gangplank, carrying the rug as if their lives depended on its safe return.

Mujod spread his hands in a gesture of apology, as if suddenly conscious of the thunderstruck group of tourists watching him. "I regret my lateness. I will be accompanying any who wish to visit the Aga Khan's mausoleum. I am ready, if you are."

"Where's Olivia?" Ford shouted over the ensuing confusion, not caring how paranoid he sounded.

"Farita, did you take Miss Cranston her breakfast this morning?" Mujod's eyes criticized the young tour guide. "Did she share her plans with you?"

Farita nodded, apparently eager to show her employer she had done her duty. "She will not be joining the group this morning. She told me she wished to rest on board the ship."

At once Mujod became his charming self again. "Fine. Fine. Now *that* is settled, I am delighted many of you have accepted my invitation for a felucca ride. Please follow me." He led a small group away to a wooden sailing boat docked next to the Emerald Empress.

Suddenly, Ford *knew* his fears were justified. There was a smell of danger in the air.

Farita motioned her group toward the gangplank.

"If Olivia isn't on board, she might have gone shopping. She told me yesterday she hadn't had time to buy anything yet," Lois offered before she followed the others out.

"Don't worry, wherever she is, I'm damn well going to find her!"

Ford's bark startled Farita. She stopped and looked back at him. "Is there any way I may be of assistance?"

Moose stepped between them and shooed the guide down the gangplank before Ford had a chance to say anything. "I will go with Farita in case Olivia has indeed gone into the town alone. I will check with you later, Ford."

Something wasn't right. Moose was deserting him. The rest of the group just going off on their own with no concern for Olivia's well-being. Even Irmentrude, who had been so solicitous of her. He shook his head to clear it, running his hands through his unbrushed hair. He probably looked like hell.

After twenty knocks on her cabin door still didn't convince him she wasn't inside, he bribed the desk clerk with a promise of a good word to the ship's owner and got the master key.

Her cabin was imbued with her unique scent, but she wasn't there. A shiver coursed down his spine. Although everything looked neat and tidy, something felt wrong. He opened her closet and fingered the clothes hung there. Every outfit she'd already worn was hanging in an orderly fashion. Nothing seemed out of place, but still he couldn't shake the strange feeling that something was terribly amiss. As his fingers trailed down the line of clothes, it came to him. There wasn't an empty hanger.

What was she wearing, then? He prowled around the cabin floor, looking under the bunk, searching the bottom of the closet, even checking in the bathroom. No empty hanger anywhere.

He returned the key to the desk and made a thorough search of the ship, moving at a steady pace from one end to the other. Finally, a heavy sensation settled in the pit of his stomach. She was nowhere to be found.

His nerves stretched to their limit, he decided he'd have to leave the ship himself. He didn't know where to look, or what to do, but somehow he would find her. Nothing and no one would stop him. After checking her cabin one last time, he started back upstairs.

"Dr. Harris, there is a call for you from Lieutenant Bey." He took the offered phone from the man behind the reception desk.

"She isn't on board, Moose." The raw edge in his voice echoed through the phone line into his ear.

"Then we have no choice but to search the town. I am at the Cataract Hotel and will start on foot toward you. Stay out of the main thoroughfares and don't ask questions, you'll just alert the wrong people. I will contact the local authorities."

Moose's orders didn't sit well with Ford. What the hell was he supposed to do? Sit around and wait?

He would not only search Aswân, he'd turn it upside down and sideways until he found her!

Ten minutes later, he was cursing the cult and Interpol for the hundredth time as he searched through the usual tourist spots along the Corniche, a broad avenue shaded by tall hibiscus trees. When that proved a waste of time, he defied Moose's edict and entered the old marketplace. The air was redolent of spices and powders, from karkade to henne, from saffron pistils to curry, from red pepper to the dark-leafed mint tea. Tall baskets overflowing with cotton in various patterns sat in the dust. If Olivia had been here, she would have stopped at this vendor. Being as discreet as possible, he described his "lady" and asked if they had seen her. But no one in the shop recognized the description.

He went on, heedless of braided straw, ebony carvings and ivory mementos that were thrust under his nose. He'd never seen so many people, and he began to imagine they were all part of the conspiracy to keep him from finding her.

Up ahead, long white galabeas fluttered in the breeze, making a rippling pattern that might hide Olivia. He ran forward, and gave her description to the overeager vendor. The shop was deep and dark, but she had never been there.

Then he noticed a rug shop. A curious feeling came over him. He searched the shop, fending off the eager salesman with promises of tomorrow. No Olivia.

Somehow, somewhere, he was missing something!

Finally, he had crisscrossed the entire tourist area of the city and had not seen a trace of her, much less Moose. How could the two of them ever find her?

He called the Empress from the elegant bar at the Cataract Hotel but there was no news. He called the headquarters of the Aswân police and found that Moose had already been there to alert them to Olivia's disappearance. Belatedly, he called the International Hospital and found out Moose had checked there, too.

So, Moose had covered all the logical places.

But logic had nothing to do with the fear ripping at him. Logic had flown out the window when Charlie disappeared. Now, had the cult taken Olivia, too?

They didn't need another hostage. He had the thet amulet for them! It was getting hard to think straight. All the unanswered questions haunted him. His only recourse was to keep searching.

He prowled the rich granite quarries on Elephantine Island, checked out the two Nubian villages and the Museum of Aswân. North of the Elephantine, on Kitchener Island, he ran into Farita with the four ladies, Lois and Irmentrude.

"Have you located Olivia yet?" they all asked eagerly.

"No." He ground out the word, his gaze scanning the botanical garden. "I thought this might be a spot she would visit."

Farita's concerned face was a study in fear. An inner fear, as if she knew something, or guessed... Ford found it hard to believe this gentle creature could have anything to do with the Osiris cult, but Moose had been acting very strangely around her.

"Of course. I shall help you search." Farita deserted the ladies who were all happily settled, sipping karkade on a terrace overlooking a tiny bay populated by white ducks. "I shall go to the east and meet you back here in thirty minutes' time." She ran, disappearing behind the bushes and disturbing the birds who lived there. They rose in protest, their squawks filling the heavy afternoon air.

Instinctively, he followed her. He'd already searched the other side, anyway, but he couldn't shake his suspicions. Bougainvillea and poinsettia, hibiscus and clematis, mango and sycamore, filled the romantic garden with pungent fragrance, but none so enticing as the scent of Olivia that he carried in his mind. Shades of color ranging from brilliant reds to delicate pinks surrounded him, but he might as well have been in the middle of the desert. Nothing mattered without Olivia.

Farita seemed thorough enough in her search. His heart banged against his ribs as he dogged her steps. He was running out of time and he knew it. When he returned to the terrace, Farita had already convinced the other ladies to leave.

"We must return to the ship and notify the authorities at once. Obviously Olivia is missing," Irmentrude bristled.

"Maybe she's already back on board," Patty offered. "She might have been shopping all day and we just missed her. It's a pretty big city."

With nowhere else to look, Ford had no choice but to accompany Farita and the six women back to the Empress. It took three of them to help Lois haul her packages. He hadn't realized how much time had passed until the city suddenly blended all of its colors into a violet sunset—sand, sky and water becoming one.

By the time he arrived on board, a murderous rage boiled in his blood. If any harm came to Olivia, he wasn't certain he could be held responsible for his actions!

The women buzzed up the gangplank, delighted to be back at home base, anxious to question if Olivia had turned up. He hung behind, trying to think of one thing he might have missed. Suddenly, he paused... maybe he had nothing to worry about. Maybe Interpol had simply decided to remove Olivia from danger. But surely, somehow, some way, they would have let him know. Surely they could see how worried he was.

Moose waited for him in the lobby, defeat written all over his face. Before Ford had a chance to offer his new theory, Akim returned. Abruptly, he remembered he had agreed to go with Akim to inspect the temple at Philae for earthquake damage.

"I have been informed by the authorities of Miss Cranston's disappearance." Akim looked at him with great sadness narrowing his face. "I am sorry, my friend. I have questioned every diplomatic contact I have in the city, to no avail."

"Despite all our efforts, it seems Olivia has just vanished." Moose looked around the group gathered in the lobby, examining each face before pausing at Farita's.

"We're wasting time here! I don't care how long it takes or if we have to scour every kilometer of Egypt and the Sudan, we're going to find her!" Raw emotion burned the back of Ford's throat.

"I fear we don't have the time for that, Ford. We need assistance."

"What about Interpol? Could they have had a hand in this?"

Moose pulled him to one side, not far from where Farita was standing. "I thought about that, too. I made a call to the highest authority and they claimed to have no knowledge of Olivia. And when I returned, I found part of the tour already dining. It appears Mr. Mujod had to leave for a business emergency, so he cut their tour across the river short."

Farita gasped, her face stiff with fear.

As if he had been waiting for just such a reaction from her, Moose whirled and grasped her arm. "What do you know about this, Farita?" Next to his muscular body, the frightened young woman looked very tiny and very vulnerable. "Tell us what you know about Olivia's disappearance."

Suddenly, there was dead silence in the lobby. A sudden flare of emotion across Farita's face gave Ford his first hope of the day.

"Let us go someplace private to speak of Mr. Mujod's absence," she said. In contrast to Moose's menacing scowl, the young guide possessed a quiet dignity.

Ford didn't give a damn about privacy, but he could see it would be necessary to pry the truth out of the guide. "We'll go up to my suite," he said.

Farita smiled at the tour group and encouraged them to go in to dinner. Despite their curiosity, most of the group moved toward the stairs, except Irmentrude.

"I demand to know what's going on. If there is any danger to us, we should be told—"

"Thank you for your concern." Ford cut her off. "I appreciate everyone who helped us search today, but there is really nothing more you can do. Please have your dinner and by then I hope we'll have some news."

As Moose pulled Farita up the stairs, Ray was coming down, cheerfully complaining to Marta about Lois's purchases. Stephen was right behind them, a disgusted expression on his face until he spied Lois and her multitude of packages.

"I say, have you located Miss Cranston yet?" Stephen asked quite casually.

Everyone and every question seemed sinister to Ford. "No, and just what do you know about it?" he barked, shifting to block Stephen's way.

"Me?" The young man shook his head and swallowed. "I haven't laid a blinkin' eye on her since last night. Been with Marta most of the day."

From the lobby, the blonde gave Ford the once-over with her cold blue eyes. "We've been sightseeing all day. It's not our place to be looking out for anybody."

"Is there anything I can do, Dr. Harris?" Ray slouched against the railing, twirling a martini glass between his fingers. "It always seemed to me Miss Cranston was an independent woman. She might just be off on her own exploring Aswân."

"Please do not worry. All will be well. Enjoy your evening." With a delicacy Ford couldn't help but admire, Farita soothed her passengers. Either she was innocent or she was damn good at subterfuge!

Once they reached his cabin and closed the door, Moose folded his arms across his chest and moved to the window, refusing to look at the young guide. Somehow, Akim had joined them. Maybe he thought his official capacity would be welcome.

Looking unsure how to begin, Farita glanced first at him, then to Moose's rigid back, and finally to the under secretary.

"Take a seat, Farita," Ford said. Although those might be the last polite words he would speak to her, he tried not to sound too threatening. He didn't want to scare her off.

Akim cleared his throat. "If there is an international incident brewing, I need to be privy to it."

"Secretary Tamarin, I assure you, Olivia's disappearance has nothing to do with Mr. Mujod." Farita's clipped words betrayed her nervousness, even more than the tight way she gripped her hands together.

"But, you aren't as sure as you once were, are you, Farita?" Moose challenged, swiveling back to her. His eyes moved slowly over her flushed face. "You have wondered, have you not, why Mr. Mujod has asked you to watch Olivia so very carefully?"

"Because she is a woman traveling alone in a country dominated by men! You should know that yourself!"

"And why did he order you to take her breakfast at so early an hour this morning?"

Farita directed such a blaze of anger at Moose, Ford saw him flinch.

"What can you tell us?" His gut twisting in a knot, Ford paced the floor in front of her. "Where has Mujod gone?"

Farita transferred her glare to him, but softened it. Obviously his opinion mattered less than Moose's. "I shall take you there myself. He would be conducting business from his home on Elephantine Island."

"I'll arrange our transportation at once." Moose's eyes lingered on Farita's face before he turned to leave the cabin.

"I fear I must accompany you."

Ford could understand Akim's concern in the face of Interpol's imminent arrival and his instructions from the ministry; but he just didn't give a damn about the Egyptian government at this moment. And he wouldn't let anyone interfere with his finding Olivia.

"I know you are worried, Dr. Harris. Fear not, we shall find her." Farita's attempt to reassure him fell flat. "In this country, a woman—any woman—is under the protection of Allah. No one will dare harm her." She rose from the chair. "Let us go. No doubt the officious Lieutenant Bey has secured transportation."

Ford led the way, running down the gangplank to the police car waiting to transport them to a nearby dock. He tried to fight against the fear that would make him less effective. He should have gotten her out of danger, insisted she return to Cairo. Somehow he managed to make this all his own fault. If only he had forced a confrontation with the cult, or insisted on knowing who the agent was. If only...

Where could she be? He clenched his fists, murderous rage pounding through his blood. Trying to think like a scientist instead of like an emotional fool, he concentrated on why Olivia had come to Egypt in the first place.

Maybe she'd had a psychic flash of Charlie and had picked up to go after him. But that made no sense to him. She wouldn't have left without contacting him somehow. Not now. Not after everything that had passed between them.

They boarded a small motorboard. In the rich moonlight glistening on the Nile, Ford could readily pick out the rocks time and the elements had carved out to resemble elephants, those sculptures that had given the tiny island its name long ago.

Farita stepped out onto the dock with confidence, directing the boatman to wait for them. She led them down a rock walk to a colonial mansion. A veranda opened out into a well-kept garden filled with flowers, their mingled fragrances cloying in the heat. The house looked dark. Ford went cold with panic until he saw the light burning in a second-floor window toward the back.

"Someone's here!" Ford breathed, urging Farita up to the entry.

She tugged on the bellpull. An overhead light flashed on and one door opened. A stoop-shouldered manservant recognized Farita, giving her a broad, toothless grin. Ford couldn't help thinking again that the tour business had done well for Mujod.

When Moose tried to take over, Farita pushed herself past him to confront the old man. "Good evening, Omir. We must see Mr. Mujod on urgent business at once."

He bowed, gesturing them into a long center hall. The walls were covered with expensive paintings. A silk oriental rug covered the pink granite floor, and a heavy mahogany sideboard filled with antique English silver took up one whole wall.

The signs were everywhere. Just as he'd felt before any other discovery he'd ever made, Ford knew they were on the right track. He restrained his need to charge up the stairs and force a confrontation.

Omir climbed the steps in what seemed to Ford slow motion.

"Soon you shall all see that I speak the truth," Farita insisted in a low voice.

Ford signaled Moose, who walked over to the sideboard to check the hallmark under an immense sterling epergne. Either Mujod came from a family of great wealth, or he had other interests besides the tour business.

Mujod appeared at the top of the stairs, an amazing red velvet robe wrapped around his short squat body. A train dragged behind him as he descended the steps like a pharaoh holding court. Ford wasn't able to read the expression on his face. Was he surprised to see them, or scared as hell?

"Farita, there is a matter of utmost importance?"

"Olivia is missing and we think you can help us find her." Ford stepped forward impatiently, anxious not to get bogged down in Egyptian hospitality.

"This is most unsettling news," Mujod said with a sigh. He didn't offer to show them to another room. "Under Secretary Tamarin, I assume the authorities have been notified. We must find Miss Cranston without provoking an international incident, which would be disastrous for the tourist trade. All my humble facilities are at your disposal."

"What is the urgent business that takes you away from the Emerald Empress and your clients?" Despite his bland expression, Moose couldn't hide his sarcasm.

It occurred to Ford that Moose had never cared for Mujod.

"Mujod Tours has business dealings with several establishments up and down the Nile which we recommend to our clients." His eyes moved slowly over their faces while he spoke, stopping finally at Farita's. "It is my duty to make sure they continue to give excellent workmanship, value and service. To that end, I must visit each establishment. Unfortunately, I have found here in Aswân some exceptions to our high standards and I have had to terminate several relationships. It is all so distressing."

The words jogged Ford's memory. "This morning, the defective carpet came from one such source?"

Mujod grimaced and buried his chin in the huge velvet collar of his robe. "Alas, I fear I can no longer recommend the Corniche Carpet Emporium to my clients." He clasped his fingers together. "Now, how may I be of further assistance to you?" he asked primly, twitching his velvet lapels. "I certainly will cooperate in the fullest with all investigations until Miss Cranston is safely restored to us."

Ford had had enough! He lunged toward Mujod, taking him by his velvet collar and peering down into his square face. "If I find out you had anything to do with Olivia's disappearance, I'll wring your fat neck with my bare hands."

Mujod's mouth fell open, emitting an odd gurgling sound.

"Come away, my friend." Ford felt Akim's strong grip on his arm. "We have done all we can here. We shall be in contact, Mr. Mujod."

Mujod backed away quickly and turned on his heel, gripping the bannister as he went up, the flamboyant robe billowing out behind him. Ford stood in the doorway watching until he disappeared.

"I don't trust him."

"Come away, Ford." Akim forced him back outside and down the steps.

Out from under the sheltering darkness of the veranda, moonlight fell on Farita's face. Something in her eyes and the way her mouth hardened in her soft face made Ford dig in his heels.

"What?" he said, his tone harsh.

"What is it, little one?" Moose softened Ford's demand using a tender tone that seemed out of character.

Farita looked at him with wonder. Then she stared out into the darkness and whispered, "Mr. Mujod told a small untruth. Those men this morning carrying the carpet were not from the Corniche Emporium. It is a family concern and I have known each father, son, uncle and cousin for years."

"That's it! They drugged her and carried her off the ship in that carpet!" Ford wouldn't let himself think of any other possibility. He whirled to go back inside to strangle the truth out of that weasel Mujod.

"Quiet!" Again Akim grabbed his arm. "Someone is coming up the path."

Moose pulled Farita against him, secreting her in the darkness beyond the scattered palm trees. Ford crouched beside Akim, muscles bunched, ready to spring into action at any provocation.

At first, he could only make out two dark silhouettes moving toward the house. The larger one seemed to be carrying some kind of bulky package.

Then the fickle moonlight came out from behind a cloud, shining like a beacon on the faces of Lois and Ray.

They were nervous, constantly looking around. When they walked by on the path, Ford could see that the burlap bag had the outline of a small statue.

Ford tensed as Lois pulled the bell and the door opened. The low-hanging roof muffled their voices. All he could make out was a soft curse from Ray as Mujod himself closed the door behind them.

Ford shifted closer. Moose rumbled low in his throat, warning him to be careful, but he didn't pay any attention.

Suddenly, Akim stood, blotting out the moon so Ford couldn't see his face.

"I fear you may be right, my friend. As a member of the Egyptian government, I feel I must search Mr. Mujod's home. There is something not right here."

Ford didn't need any more encouragement. He launched himself at the door.

Chapter Nine

Ford was ready to knock down the whole damn house if he had to! Adrenaline coursing through his veins, he slammed into the door with his right shoulder.

The wide wooden door groaned, but remained closed. He stepped back to storm the barrier again.

"Wait!" Moose came up behind him, shouting. "On two, Ford!"

Ford looked over at his friend and something passed between the two men. In sync, they stepped back, took a deep breath and propelled themselves forward at the same moment.

The door was no match for their combined weight. It flew open.

Ford sprinted into the hall. Off to the left, in a sitting room, Lois shrieked, and Mujod, still in his opulent robe, rose from his seat in shock. Ray, standing across the room, went for his pocket.

"Stop!" Moose bellowed, "Police!" A gun appeared in his hand and pointed straight at Ray's chest.

Ford took a step toward Mujod. The little man stepped back, then in a flash he whipped a golden statue out of Lois's lap and disappeared into the paneling behind him.

"Secret passage!" Ford yelled, rushing out into the hall to look for his escape route. Mujod could be anywhere in the house. After a few minutes he rushed back into the room, his search for the man an exercise in futility. Mujod could be anywhere.

All the color draining from her face, Farita's hands trembled as she leaned against the wall for support. Akim strode across the room and contemplated the bookshelves for a few moments while Moose cuffed Ray. Then Akim ran his hands along the paneling, looking for the release lever.

"Did you see what he took, Ford?" the under secretary asked.

For a moment, Ford had to stop and think. He had been concentrating so hard on finding Olivia that the flash of gold had hardly registered. He met Akim's wide dark eyes thoughtfully. "The statue of Ament! It was stolen from a private collector in England three months ago."

Ford visualized Charlie's notes: the block of stone containing a portion of the Book of the Dead, the statue, the amulet—all necessary for the resurrection of the dead. Finally, the pieces were falling into place and Ford didn't like it one bit.

"I am a legitimate antiquities dealer," Ray shouted as Lois cried in loud gulping sobs.

"The authorities will be most interested to hear it." Moose reached into Ray's pocket and pulled out a small handgun. "Akim, call the Aswân police."

Ford grabbed Ray, shaking him as a terrier would a bone. "Where is Olivia?"

Moose tried to pull his friend away, but Ford was beside himself with fear. These crazy cult people could have done anything with her.

Ray broke down. "Honestly, I don't know anything. I just came here to sell the statue to Mr. Mujod."

Ford swore, short and sweet. He turned to the doorway to find that the manservant had appeared and was whispering to Farita.

"Where is she?" he bellowed at the servant. "The beautiful young woman that your master brought to his house this morning!" Ford stopped in the doorway, towering over the intimidated servant who fluttered his hands ineffectually.

Finally, he pointed a shaky finger toward the second floor.

Ford flew up the steps three at a time, his heart pounding. Had he made another mistake? Had he waited too long downstairs? Had Mujod run off and taken her hostage?

"Olivia! Olivia! Where are you?" He would tear the house apart, piece by piece, if he had to, to find her!

The first door opened into a grandiose bedchamber reminiscent of a pharaoh's treasure room. It was full of priceless antiquities—priceless and stolen. Moose would get high praise for busting this guy.

He went back into the hall and called her name again and again as he threw open doors.

"OLIVIA! Olivia! Where are you?" A familiar, compelling voice broke into the peaceful world where she floated, unaware of her surroundings. She tried to rouse herself and found it was much easier to give in to the insistent tranquillity of the drugs.

"Olivia! Olivia!"

Too exhausted, she deliberately shut the voice out. Her fuzzy brain, which demanded rest, was unable to tether itself to anything real.

A crash echoed in the distance and light invaded her darkened bower.

"Olivia!"

Ford! Her mind screamed his name in relief, but she still couldn't move.

"Akim, I found her! Get me some tea! Fast!" His voice demanded her attention. "Wake up! Speak to me!"

She felt herself being lifted gently, her robe settling around her. Ford's strong arm kept her upright as she sagged against his side. She moaned.

"Wake up. Do it for me, love."

She forced her heavy eyelids open.

His arm tightened. "That's it, love. Stay with me." He raised her to her feet, supporting her weight entirely. "Come on, Olivia. Fight it! Walk with me."

He forced her to try to take a few steps but her body refused to obey. She stumbled.

"Where in hell is that tea?" he shouted. He seemed to be very angry with her, but that was nothing new. He was always either charming or angry, but she found she had begun to crave both.

Someone else came into the room but Olivia was too disoriented to identify who it was. A cup was thrust under her lips.

"Drink this." Ford was insistent, his voice a deep rasping plea.

Her lips felt dry and cracked, as if she hadn't had water for days. She could barely manage to open them.

"Drink!" he demanded.

For his sake she tried to swallow, but most of the liquid spilled down her chin. He made her take another step, then stopped and forced her to drink.

After a few moments, she began to feel again. Her head hurt and her body protested. He shoved the cup under her lips again. She shook her head, despite the pain.

"What is it?" she croaked through a throat parched by thirst.

"Mint tea." He lifted her head, urging her to drink.

Finally, she took a good draft. The liquid soothed her aching throat going down. It hit her empty stomach and turned around to come up again.

"I'm going to be sick!" She turned away, her head swimming and her insides lurching like a ship in heavy seas.

"That's the idea. You've got to get the drug out of your system." Ford hauled her toward a small bathroom.

She hadn't been sick since she was a small child and never in front of anyone. But it only seemed right that he was there, his soothing hands and low voice a source of support and comfort.

Afterward, he bathed her sweating face and body with warm water. Like a child, she obeyed his instructions to lift her arms so he could peel off her dirty robe, and then again when he slipped a cool, sweet-smelling galabea over her head.

"Feeling better now?"

She nodded, content to let Ford take care of her for the moment. "Where are we?"

"Mujod's house on Elephantine Island."

"I need to sit down."

He sat on the edge of an immense iron tub and pulled her onto his lap, holding her as if it were the most important thing he had to do.

Gradually, it all came back to her, the horrible feeling of being out of control, as if her body had betrayed her. Then that one split second before she passed out when she'd seen Mujod in Ford's room, the thet amulet in his hand.

"Ford, Mujod is the cult member!" She grabbed the front of his shirt, holding on for dear life. "He stole the thet amulet from your cabin. They aren't going to bargain for Charlie at all! We have to find him."

"Easy, love. We will. I promise you." He kissed her forehead and she sighed, too exhausted to argue with him.

From the doorway a voice asked, "How is she?" She swung her head up from his shoulder to see Akim silhouetted in the doorway.

Not comfortable with her vulnerable position, she swayed to her feet. "Where is Mr. Mujod? Under arrest?"

"We are searching the house for him. There may be a tunnel out into the grounds. The police have arrived."

"We have to find him! He's the only one who can lead us to my brother!" Ford grabbed for her arm, trying to stop her, but she refused to give in to weakness and stumbled into the bedroom.

"Damn it, Olivia, you are the stubbornest woman I've ever met," he muttered angrily. A supportive arm curled around her shoulders.

"Thank you." She glanced around at her opulent surroundings, taking in the richness of the fabrics, the age of the furniture, the elegance of the appointments.

A short while later, Ford and Akim stood on either side of her, supporting her as she made her way down the staircase and across the hall. She came face-to-face with Lois and Ray, who were being escorted out by the Aswân police. They both wore handcuffs.

Taking a great gulping breath, Lois blinked at Olivia from swollen eyes and tried to explain. "We just wanted to sell our statue. Mr. Mujod said he could arrange it, so we took this tour. Nobody's ever gotten hurt before." She tried to reach out to Olivia but the policeman pulled her away. "I never dreamed something like this would happen. Oh, Ray!" She sobbed into her hands.

"Shut up, Lois!" Ray glared at them over his shoulder as two police officers led them away.

Stunned, Olivia stared at their retreat. "Ray and Lois are members of the cult?" Maybe the drug hadn't completely left her system; none of this made sense to her.

"I believe that Ray is an international player, Olivia," Akim answered in his calm soothing voice. "Someone contacted him, he made certain contacts and the statue came into his possession. I believe he had no other involvement than the passing of the Ament to Mr. Mujod."

She turned frightened eyes to Ford and realized he had already remembered. The statue of Ament had been mentioned in Charlie's notes as a necessity for the resurrection ceremony.

She began to shake.

What could all this mean to Charlie? Now she was frightened that Mujod or the rest of the cult might retaliate in some dreadful way.

Moose rushed into the hall, leading Farita by the hand. She sobbed, her face ravaged by her tears. "Oh, thank goodness, you are unharmed."

But Farita had brought her the drugged tea. How could she be helping Ford?

Ford wasn't paying any attention to Farita now. Instead, he had homed in on the manservant sitting quietly against the wall on the floor. "We must find your master."

The old man began to quiver in reaction.

"Where has he gone?"

He whispered something Olivia couldn't quite catch. Farita questioned him sternly before turning to report, "He's making a run for it on the Nile!"

Ford bounded forward, suddenly issuing orders. "I'll follow him. Moose, you take Olivia back to the ship and keep her in your sight at all times."

Everyone seemed to expect her to acquiesce to this absurd plan. Ford was already half out the door and Moose and Farita were coming to her assistance when she blurted out, "No!"

Ford turned from the doorway. "Must you always be so stubborn?"

"I'm going with you. Charlie's out there somewhere and he needs me!"

"Yes, you must go." Unexpectedly, Akim took charge. "I will report this to the ministry and have them alert Interpol. Somehow you must leave word of your destination. You may need reinforcements!"

Olivia was ready. She sprinted out the door, urging Ford to hurry. Moose gave Akim instructions about the old man and took off after them, with Farita trailing him. Their launch was long gone, but a felucca was tied up nearby, the captain rolling his sail. Moose negotiated an enormous sum for the craft and they cast off within minutes. Ahead, hardly visible, another white sail moved toward the east bank.

Farita pulled binoculars out of her large purse. "It is Mr. Mujod. See, there, near the top of the mast is the tour emblem on a small flag." She handed the binoculars to Ford.

There was no chance they could catch him, but Ford urged the captain to increase his speed. With the sail trimmed a bit, the boat heeled and soon they were clipping up the Nile faster than Olivia would have thought possible. She strained to follow the movements of the ship ahead.

Ford stood in the prow, helping the captain navigate. They glided past Philae, where Isis's temple raised its columns and pillars toward a star-filled sky.

Suddenly, he turned to Moose. "I've never been this far upriver. What can we expect?"

"We are approaching the First Cataract of the Nile, a vast zone of turbulent waters and whirlpools. We won't be able to go much farther."

Farita gripped the edge of the boat, her knuckles showing white in the moonlight as the craft lurched in the treacherous waters. Ford continued to stand, bracing himself against the mast.

"There." He gestured. "Mujod has put ashore. I can see the sail luffing."

Slowly, too slowly, they approached the same dock. Moose brushed past the captain, jumped ashore and helped Farita off the boat. Ford, too, was off the small vessel before it even docked. Olivia stood and the felucca rocked violently.

"Take my hand." Ford extended a steadying arm and plucked her off the moving boat.

She caught a glimpse of Mujod running toward a small group of buildings. But by the time they reached a dirt crossroads, he was out of sight.

Ford and Moose shared a string of curses but Farita motioned them to be quiet and disappeared into what was no more than a shack with several cars parked in the front yard.

"Can we trust her?" Olivia's suspicions were mounting by the moment.

"Definitely." Moose's confident reply was something of a surprise. "She helped us find Mujod's house."

Farita returned, dangling a set of keys. "We have a car. I know the drivers here from some of my earlier tours. But we must hurry. Mujod started into the desert. If he gets too far ahead, we will never find him. My friends will report to the captain of the Emerald Empress that we are following him into the desert."

She led them to a low, black car, which had the distinction of looking like a hearse. Moose grabbed the keys. "I have more experience than you in tailing cars."

In no time, they were out of the village and on a paved road heading east into the Nubian night.

"There's nothing between the Nile and the Red Sea, unless Mujod is headed for Berenice. He might be able to get a small plane out of the country," Ford said through tight lips.

Olivia tried to stay calm. Surely Charlie wasn't out in this vast wasteland. Behind them, to the north, the Nile gleamed like a string of diamonds. The car was climbing long sweeping curves of road that led into a measureless dark.

Suddenly Farita gasped. The taillights of a car ahead came into view. Without speaking, Moose slowed. He switched off his own headlights and kept the lights ahead just within sight.

Olivia made an involuntary sound of protest.

"No sense in scaring him off," Ford muttered. "He's going into the Sudan."

The words echoed in the dark silence. Olivia glanced at Moose's sharp profile, then at Ford's. Did he know where Mujod was heading? Why didn't somebody say something?

As if sensing her distress, Ford took her hand and pressed it to his lips. "He's not going toward Berenice."

He kept hold of her hand while leaning over the seat to speak very quietly to Moose. "There's nothing to the southeast of Aswân—no oasis that I can think of. Do you know where he might be going?"

Moose thought for a while, then shook his head. "All we can do is follow."

Olivia sent prayers to any god who might listen as they sped through the Egyptian night and focused her thoughts on Charlie. If he was out here, he would have to know she was coming to him. Maybe, just maybe, he could send her a sign.

Always careful to stay out of sight of the car ahead, they finally had to leave the paved road and drive even slower along a rough desert track. The shocks in the car had long ago given out, making it a rough ride.

There was really nothing to mark the way. Moose seemed to be going on instinct, occasionally swerving to miss a pale gray rock in the center of the road. All around, outside the car, it looked like a moonscape.

Where was Mujod headed? Did he have any idea they were right behind him?

She could sense the tension level in the car begin to rise. Everyone knew what was at stake. She could see for miles ahead, but there was nothing except the intermittent winking of Mujod's taillights. This barren land was carved into small hillocks, with canyons, gullies and ravines that looked impossible for human habitation. Yet she had read that nomads still lived and herded in this desert, as they had done for thousands of years.

Ahead, a small rise obscured Mujod's car. Moose gunned the engine. Relieved, Olivia saw the taillights again as soon as they crested the hill.

They swept down into a valley, then up another hillock. When they cleared this one, the taillights were gone. Cursing, his profile turned to stone, Moose accelerated until the car shook from the speed. They all craned forward, their eyes searching for a light, a movement . . . anything!

Farita's soft sobs tore through Olivia like a barrage of bullets. She knew, they all knew that they had lost Mujod.

"We can't give up! Go on!" she cried. In the darkness she searched for Ford's hand and found it, gripping it like a lifeline. "Please, you all must help me find Charlie."

He met her eyes and the understanding she read in his gaze made the pain inside her break apart. "Keep going, Moose. We'll pick up a trail somehow."

In silence they drove for mile after mile, the terrain so uniform, they might have been traveling in endless circles, for all she knew.

"Stop!" Olivia shouted.

Moose slammed on the brakes. The long black car skidded on the loose sand and finally came to a halt facing back the way they'd come.

For some unknown reason, Olivia felt compelled to get out of the car. She stared into the desert until her eyes burned. She couldn't make anything out of the oddly shaped rocks and shifting sands. What had come over her? Why did she, who knew nothing of this land, think they should stop right here?

"What is it, Olivia?" Ford's soft voice held sympathy and understanding.

She shook her head in frustration.

"We have been searching the desert for hours. I fear it is hopeless." Moose got out of the car and stretched. "There is nothing here, Olivia."

Farita rolled down her window. "I wish I knew where Mr. Mujod has gone," she repeated as she had over and over in the past hour. "If only I had allowed myself to trust my instincts sooner."

"Why didn't you?" Moose asked in a strangely gentle tone.

Farita stepped out of the car and stared at him, dumbfounded. "Mr. Mujod has been a friend of my family's for many years. By working for him, I have been able to finish my degree at Alexandria University. Before this, he has shown me only kindness. I did not see beyond that facade. I regret I am not so keen a judge of human nature as I once believed."

Against the pale light in the night sky, Farita and Moose were only dark silhouettes, but Olivia didn't need to see them any clearer. Somehow she knew this was their moment of truth. To give them privacy, she climbed back into the car. Ford followed her, spreading open a map he found in the glove compartment.

"Here is the route we've just covered," he said. "We really are out in the middle of nowhere."

She couldn't bear to look into his eyes and see defeat. She glanced out at that desert, seeking answers.

The clouds opened for a moment, allowing the moon to throw grotesque shadows against the sand. Up ahead, a peculiar formation caught her attention.

"Ford, what's that?" Following her direction, he stared out into the night.

He shot out the door, racing toward the odd shape. She sprinted after him, hanging on to his arm as the sand pulled on her ankles.

"What is it?"

"It's a burial mound, the kind only used in southern Egypt."

Olivia heard the car start up and Farita called, "It is much farther away than it looks. Please, come inside."

Together, they trekked back to the car and got in. "Keep the headlights off and don't get too close." Ford's voice sounded loud in the heavy silence.

Olivia kept her eyes fixed on the sand mound ahead as it grew larger and larger in the windshield. Moose finally stopped the car. Swiveling, he met Ford's eyes with a significant glance.

She didn't need anyone to tell her they'd found what they'd been looking for.

Before they got out of the car, Ford and Moose disabled the interior lights. Careful not to make a sound that might carry in the still desert air, all four of them crept out of the car.

Voices drifted across the sand, loud voices that didn't care if they were heard. Ford dropped to his knees and motioned them down beside him.

Some unspoken signal passed between the men. Moose knelt over Farita, whispering close to her ear.

Turning to Olivia, Ford cupped her face with strong fingers. "For once, do what I ask and stay put. Moose and I have to check to see how many guards Mujod has posted."

Her answer was a quick kiss pressed to his mouth. He stared at her for one second more before both he and Moose dropped onto their bellies and inched toward the mound in opposite directions.

Olivia stayed put. Her body made a hollow in the cold sand. Beside her, Farita stayed perfectly still. It felt as if the world held its breath, waiting.

A strange clicking sound that was definitely out of place in all this endless quiet sounded behind her. She turned to look. Although she knew nothing about guns, she'd seen enough television to recognize a deadly weapon when she saw one.

Two guards aimed some sort of rifle straight into her face.

Steadily she rose to her feet. If they were going to shoot her, she wasn't going to die groveling in the sand.

From out of nowhere Ford materialized, pushing her behind his own body, standing between her and certain death.

A soft voice, a voice she recognized only too well, came from out of the night. "Welcome to your burial chamber."

Chapter Ten

Farita sobbed softly, shrinking into Moose's embrace as Mujod and two guards leveled rifles at them. Olivia could feel Ford's tension, and realized that he was measuring the guards' courage as well as their size. One loomed a few inches taller than both Ford and Moose, who were about the same height, and the other was shorter but looked physically powerful.

Olivia didn't want him to take any chances—not with the guns pointed directly at them; not while she still hadn't found Charlie.

"No." Her breathy whisper could only have reached Ford's ears.

He squeezed her hand reassuringly. "So you were my contact all along, Mujod." He sounded calm enough, but pressed up against his body she could feel that he was anything but calm. "I thought we had a deal. The thet amulet in return for Charlie."

"Alas, arrangements change. We did not know that Miss Cranston would be a constant impediment to a private meeting. And so, new arrangements have been made. It seems Olivia will be a vital part of what will occur here."

Mujod's chilly smile froze her blood. How could she contribute anything to the cult? All she wanted was her brother safely returned.

"Take her!"

On Mujod's command, the taller guard lunged toward her. Ford moved quickly and she found herself thrust an arm's length behind him.

He raised his fists menacingly. "You and all your guards will have to go through me first!"

Moose shifted his body closer, making a human wall of protection in front of Olivia and Farita.

"I fear that is part of your destiny." Mujod shrugged, as if they were having a normal conversation. "I am not a cruel man. I simply wish to take Olivia to her brother. After all, is that not the reason you have all followed me here?"

The hope of seeing her brother proved stronger than her fear. She pushed Farita out of her way and stepped forward willingly. "Is Charlie here?"

"I will take you to him now." Almost compassionately, the tour owner held out his hand toward her. "Come."

"No! She's not going anywhere with you!" Ford stepped forward and grabbed her shoulders.

"If you do not release her, I will simply have you shot, Dr. Harris. It makes no difference to me if you die now, or later."

Terror roared in her ears, and with all her strength she threw herself away from the safe haven of Ford's arms.

"I want to see my brother. Right now." She could hear her voice breaking. Her heart was splintering from the choice she had to make. She took another step forward and felt the pressure of Ford's hands on her shoulders. Turning to face him, she stared into his anguished face and mouthed the words, "Stay alive."

Moose reached out to restrain him and she turned away. Mr. Mujod took her arm, leading her into the darkness. The desert wind blew hot particles of sand through the thin gauzy galabea that skimmed her body. The moon hung low in the western sky and inky night shrouded the barren landscape. She had no idea where she was being taken, but that didn't matter as long as she found Charlie.

She dragged her feet, turning to look back at Ford and Moose and Farita. Their silhouettes and those of the guards holding them prisoner offered her no encouragement. She stumbled in the sand and Mujod yanked her back on her feet with a surprisingly strong grip.

It seemed as if they'd walked forever when he stopped in front of a mound of sand and rock. There was nothing special or beautiful about it, and she never would have singled it out as anything but a natural formation. But another narrow-faced guard stood in front of it, a rifle slung low on his hip.

Seemingly out of nowhere, he exposed an entrance to the south and she saw a crude stone ramp descending into the bowels of the earth.

Olivia wasn't claustrophobic, but she had a hard time going into the narrow opening. She had to bend double and often her elbows scraped the walls on either side of her. If it weren't for Charlie, she never would have made it to the bottom.

When they reached the end of the passageway, all three of them crowding into a chamber carved into the heart of the rock, she couldn't breathe. The air was flat and dry and deoxygenated.

She gasped.

"Breathe slowly, Miss Cranston," Mujod ordered. "There's plenty of air for now."

The guard climbed to the roof by means of cleverly concealed stone hand- and foot-holds. He slid back a slab to reveal another chamber and let a rope down.

"Tie this around your waist. I'll be right behind you, so do not attempt to resist." For the first time, Olivia realized Mujod had a gun pointed at her back.

The man with the thin face pulled her up whenever she couldn't reach the handhold, and Mujod pushed from behind. If she wasn't absolutely terrified, she would have been embarrassed because she wore nothing beneath the thin dress. Just when she was certain she couldn't have taken another step, even with a gun pointed at her, she finally reached the ceiling and was pulled into another small chamber.

The passage leading out of this room was choked with debris—every size of stone from tiny shards to gigantic blocks.

"Observe, Miss Cranston," Mujod said when he joined her. "Some thief thousands of years ago laboriously chiseled a tunnel through that stone but it was a dead end." He pushed the gun into the small of her back, urging her forward.

Above her, she could feel tons of dirt and stone pressing down. She kept repeating the same refrain over and over in her mind—this mound had stood for thousands of years, there was no reason to believe it would fall in on her.

When they reached the next chamber, even her captors were beginning to gasp for breath. It felt as if all the oxygen had been used and reused until there was no life-giving property left in it. Mujod jammed the gun painfully into her side, forcing her to move deeper and deeper into the heart of the mound.

After what seemed like an eternity, they reached another trapdoor. Apparently, the ancients had trusted no one. This time they dropped down into a passage.

"You see how clever my ancient ancestors were when they created this burial chamber. The far side of the passage is filled with stone in order to suggest the burial chamber lies beyond it. But it's right here, in the middle!"

Mujod pushed her into a space no larger than a cubbyhole. She had to wriggle through about ten feet before it opened into a larger area and she could stand. Olivia looked around in surprise. The large granite room was hand-hewn from solid rock, yet strangely enough, she could feel fresh air. She took great gulps of it into her lungs, trying to stave off some of her fear.

Suddenly, she smelled incense, the same odor that had awakened her aboard the Emerald Empress. In the corner, a small brazier burned below a crude altar.

Her brother stepped out of the shadows, shock blazing from eyes so identical to her own. "Olivia?"

He needed a haircut, a shave and a bath, but Olivia was so overjoyed to see him alive and in one piece, she didn't care. She flew into his arms.

"Charlie, thank God you're alive!"

He held her at arm's length, disbelief hardening his face. "I can't believe this! What are you doing here?"

"I sensed you were in trouble, so I came to help, just like always. Six minutes behind at birth and I've been right behind you ever since." She tried to joke with him but in reality she was shocked at his appearance. He looked tired and hungry, which was to be expected, but as she stared into his eyes, she also saw defeat. She'd never known Charlie to give up on anything.

He put his arms around her and buried his face in her hair. "I'm sorry, Olivia. This time we're in a real mess."

Over his shoulder she gazed around at the painted wall reliefs that covered every inch of the chamber. "Where are we?"

"Allow me to answer you, Miss Cranston."

Charlie released her and they both turned and faced their captor. Supremely confident with the armed guard behind him, Mujod had holstered his gun.

"This is the tomb of an Egyptian governor of the south who was buried before the first dynasty. If you will notice the drawings, you will see that his ceremony was much different than the kings and queens in the Valley. He was buried with the bodies of his Nubian harem around him."

Her heart pumped erratically. Was this what Ford had tried to warn her about? No! It must be another of this madman's attempts to terrify her. "I thought it was common knowledge that Egyptians didn't make human sacrifices. If you're trying to frighten me, you're doing a lousy job of it! You should stick to tour directing, or stealing!"

"Actually, Olivia, he's telling the truth this time," Charlie said softly. "Egyptologists used to be smug about the civilized habits of their people, until a tomb uncovered at Kerma revealed the bodies of several hundred people, most of them women and children who had been buried alive with their dead king."

She stared at her brother in disbelief. Even in the midst of this horrifying captivity, he still had to be a scientist, laboriously explaining the truth instead of lying to reassure her!

"Ah...such a fascinating discovery." Mujod's chilly little smile froze her with terror. "I've read the accounts. Some of the sacrificed lay with their faces hidden in their hands or protected by a bent arm. One poor girl had crawled under the bed in which her dead lord rested. That act must have prolonged the agony of death by suffocation. Such a painful way in which to leave this world. I would not wish it to happen to one as lovely as you, Miss Cranston."

The smug way he was baiting them infuriated her. She wouldn't be afraid of this little man! Healthy anger gave her new courage.

She threw up her head in a gesture of defiance. "I don't know what stupid games you're playing, but I've had enough of them! I demand you release us at once!"

Mujod's grimace reminded her of a spoiled child. "It is not written to be so, Miss Cranston. This mound was found hundreds of generations ago by a powerful family. They have secretly buried their dead here and they *believe* in the old magic. The power of this place will be unleashed once the Osiris sarcophagus is opened."

"You're crazy!" She stepped away from the fanatical light in his eyes, shaking with anger. How could this be happening? New terror sucked the courage away from her. She could barely whisper her brother's name. "Charlie, what is this madman talking about?"

He turned toward her and placed his hands on her shoulders to reassure her. With a soft command, Mujod sent the guard out into the cramped passageway. She shrank into the warmth of Charlie's embrace.

"I assure you, Miss Cranston, I am not mad." Mujod suddenly looked uneasy. "If there is madness here, it comes from others. My motivation is greed, pure and simple."

He gestured around the room. "This in itself was a great find, but there was nothing here I could sell. And then your precious Charlie stumbled onto the greatest find of all time, a prize I couldn't resist. So you must open the Osiris box. Until then, I fear you will remain here without food or water."

"I promised you a prize worthy even to one as greedy as you, Mujod. But the puzzle is complicated and I need more time," Charlie said briskly, his fingers pressing into her tense shoulders.

"You have had time, Dr. Cranston. My patience grows thin. The sand in the hourglass is running out, not only for you but, alas, for my other uninvited guests, as well."

"No! Don't hurt them!" Olivia turned on Mujod, her fingers curling involuntarily, wanting to scratch out his eyes. "Tell me what you want. Maybe I can help."

"Easy, Olivia," Charlie said calmly. Only the strength of her brother's hands kept her from launching herself at Mujod. "I'll show you."

He pulled her away, but she refused to turn her back on the tour director. Charlie tugged her to the altar, which she saw was only a shelf cut into the rock face.

A jewel-encrusted miniature sarcophagus glistened a dozen brilliant colors of lapis, carnelian and gold. The design work was so extraordinarily beautiful, she couldn't resist taking the casket into her own hands.

"Remember I wrote you about the digger, Omar, and the legend passed down through his family? It was all true, Olivia! By working with the texts in certain of the monuments, I developed a theory. Even Ford didn't believe me but I was right! I found it! The treasure of a lifetime—the left hand of Osiris!" A small flame lit his eyes.

Nothing mattered but the find. She couldn't quite take it all in. Even now, nothing was important to Charlie—not her, not Ford, or the others waiting below, not even his own life—only that treasure.

"But, Charlie, Ford says..."

"He's wrong. Inside that casket rests the golden hand of Osiris, placed there by Isis thousands upon thousands of years ago."

Tension quivered in the air, making it difficult to breathe normally. She glanced at Mujod, reassuring herself that he hadn't left to issue some unthinkable order about Ford and the others. "Isn't that whole story just a myth?"

"Ford and most other archaeologists think so." Under the scraggly growth of beard, his mouth twisted in a smile. "I can't wait to show them I was right all along. I risked my life to find it. That damn earthquake nearly buried it again, and me. If it hadn't been for the cult members following me, who pulled me out in time, I would have been a goner.''

Dazed, Olivia studied her brother's set face. ''What do they want from you?''

''They want me to open the casket, but I can't. It's a puzzle box.'' He took it from her hands, to hold it out in front of him, turning it over and over. ''I've been working on it, and I'd open it in a second if I could.''

''Now you have your chance, Miss Cranston. I fear our time here is running out. I would not wish to wait here for more unwelcome visitors. You have two hours.'' Mujod's voice was steady and resigned.

Mujod didn't care if he had to sacrifice them all for his own greed. She felt a faint stab of hope when he disappeared into the black hole they had come through, but the grinding noise of the trapdoor sealing them in made her knees buckle. She slumped against Charlie.

''What are we going to do?''

''Get out of this alive!'' He gave her a quick, fierce hug. ''Now tell me, how did you get here? How did you ever get tangled up with the cult?''

''I followed Ford after I saw him steal the thet amulet from the museum. It was the price they demanded for your release, but I didn't find that out until we reached Luxor.''

For a moment he looked dazed. ''You followed Ford from Cairo to Luxor? Then how did you end up here?''

''It's too long a story to explain now. But Ford and I ended up following Mujod to find you.'' She grabbed the torn edges of her brother's filthy shirt. ''We've got to stall them! They have Ford and Moose and my guide, Farita. I'm afraid they might kill them all before help can arrive. Ford notified Interpol right away, and Akim Tamarin from the Antiquities Ministry is going to put them onto our trail."

"We have two hours before the cult does anything drastic. Do you think you can open the box, Olivia? Maybe I've been staring at it so long, I can't see the forest for the trees." He fell to his knees beside the altar. "Here, take a look."

For better light, she took two of the four oil lamps that lit the chamber and placed them on either side of her. The precious box was even more beautiful lit by lamplight. Whoever had designed this had left no trace of hinge, mechanism or lid. The unbroken lines of gold and jewels melded into a seamless puzzle.

A shiver ran down her spine. She looked around. Charlie was exhausted and now that she was here, his body was beginning to give out. He rested his head against the wall, his eyelids fluttering shut. Dark shadows marked his face and she could see bruises on his arms and legs. What had these people done to him?

A new fear ripped through her. It was up to her now. Up to her to save Charlie and Ford and Farita and Moose. She bent over the box, determination flowing through her veins. Somehow she had to get them all out of this!

After a half hour of study had given her no clue at all, she stretched her neck, seeking to ease the tension. She looked up into the shadows, searching for inspiration. An eerie feeling that the eyes painted on the walls were staring back at her taunted her.

Stop being stupid and get to work, she ordered her muddled brain. Taking short rapid breaths, she forced all her attention onto the jeweled box. Discipline had always been her bulwark. Her entire life she'd depended on persistence and ingenuity.

But she couldn't keep her mind on her task. Instead, thoughts of Ford kept distracting her. Where was he? Was he all right? Would she ever see him again?

Angrily she shook her head, dashing her knuckles against her eyes to wipe away the tears forming there. For the first time in her life, she wished she had a bond with someone other than her twin. If she did, she'd open her heart and mind to call to Ford.

IGNORING THE GUARD'S rifle rammed into his side, Ford stopped and lifted his head. He could swear he heard Olivia calling his name! He twisted around, his eyes searching the darkness. Where had that bastard Mujod taken her?

"Damn it, where is Olivia?" He spat the words at his captor in defiance of the gun pointed at him.

The next second he lay flat on the sand, his jaw throbbing from the blow of the guard's rifle butt.

Moose hauled him to his feet, shielding him with his body. "Think with your head, not your heart. We have to come up with a plan."

Moose's urgent whisper got through to him. Stilling the urge to launch himself at the guards, Ford allowed himself to be pushed forward into a rough hut. As was his custom, he looked at the room, gauging his surroundings. Details were always the answer. Right now he needed to find a way to get away from these guards. Along with Moose and Farita, he had been put in a squalid, dark room barely lit by a smoking oil lamp. A collection of large lumpy pillows with rough burlap thrown over them dispensed a distinct odor of goats. Beside them was a rough wooden table holding an earthenware pitcher, two cups and a bowl. When he lifted the pitcher, he discovered it was empty and too light to be used as a weapon.

"Come, look at this!" He whirled at the excitement in Moose's voice.

He hadn't noticed a door set into the opposite side of the room where the wall was all shadows. It rattled when yanked on, but wouldn't give, no matter how hard he pulled.

"That could be a way out for us." He began to pace the small area, and Farita shrank into a corner seemingly trying to stay out of his way. All logic was deserting him in his overwhelming need to find Olivia. "Moose, I've got to get out of here. If you could just think of some diversion..."

"You will never find her where I have placed her, Dr. Harris." Mujod appeared in the doorway they had entered through.

In two steps he could have his hands around that fat throat but that wouldn't help him find Olivia. He had to wait and discover what kind of a game Mujod was playing. Moose took a menacing step forward, and there was a momentary flash of fear in Mujod's eyes before he slammed the door shut between them and him.

"I am not a cruel man." Even through the wood Ford could hear the mockery in Mujod's voice. "So I'll tell you, Miss Cranston has at last been reunited with her beloved brother. They hold in their hands your destiny. Pray that they succeed in their task or in less than an hour, I regret I must bid you all farewell."

Ford pounded his hand against the wall in frustration. When he looked around, he was surprised to find Moose standing beside Farita as if he could shelter her from harm. Unfortunately, not even his physical power would stand up against automatic weapons.

"We've got an hour to come up with something," Ford said grimly.

"Perhaps by then, Interpol will have arrived." Farita seemed to gather strength from Moose's proximity. "My friends should have alerted the ship hours ago that we came into the desert."

A tug of admiration for Farita's newfound courage made Ford smile at Moose.

At last Moose's feelings overruled his innate reserve; he bent over and pressed a kiss to Farita's smooth forehead. "Do not be afraid, little one. You are right. Help will be arriving at any moment."

Feeling like a fifth wheel, Ford turned away to give them some privacy. At the same time, he picked up the clay pitcher and smashed it on the edge of the rough wooden table, cracking it. After some persuasion, he was able to break it into fairly even pieces. Taking one, he began to chip away at the wood surrounding the latch on the rough plank door.

This door was the one thing that might lead to freedom and Olivia.

After a few moments, Moose and Farita joined him. There seemed to be an agreement between them but Ford didn't ask any questions. For a moment, he enjoyed the glow of Farita's face and the strange vulnerability surrounding his old friend.

Within twenty minutes, they had gouged out several large chunks of wood.

"Stand back and pray this works." Ford took a deep breath and alongside Moose put his shoulder to the door. They shoved.

The door didn't budge. Taking a step back, careful to make no sound, they pushed against the door again. It groaned and Farita gave the thumbs-up sign. Turning around to use the other shoulder, Ford smiled encouragingly at his friend. Moose put both hands against the wood.

"Now," Ford commanded.

The door gave way, although the latch held. It seemed their strength had split the planking at a sensitive spot, giving them just enough room to slip through.

They found another room, much different than the hovel they had been in. Rich rugs adorned the walls and a lush Egyptian carpet covered the dirt floor. Scattered about were large pillows and several chests. In one they found a heavy brass tea set and large copper plates.

"Leave it to Mujod to surround himself with luxury even in the middle of the desert," Ford muttered. "Take a weapon."

He'd been right. The door had led to just what he needed.

Moose took up two of the copper plates, hefting them in his large hands, judging their weight before adding a third. Ford couldn't resist choosing the large teapot.

"What shall I take?" Farita asked.

Ford shook his head. "I have another job for you. C'mon!"

He raced into the hut, followed by Moose and Farita, and pressed his ear to the outer door. He could hear the voices of the guards, but not Mujod's. They were laughing at some unknown jest. He strained to catch bits and pieces of their conversation and at last understood what the joke was. Rage boiled up inside him. He turned to Moose, who laid a restraining hand on his arm.

"They've sealed Olivia in the tomb."

Farita bit her lip so hard it bled. She backed away from the door, her eyes rounding into two large circles. She looked to Moose for support but he had no words of comfort to give her.

Ford walked across the room, took her hand and pulled her toward the door. "On the count of three, I want you to start screaming. Don't stop till I tell you," he whispered next to her ear.

Moose took up a position on one side of the door, his legs braced apart for action.

"One. Two." Ford mounted the words. "Three!"

Farita's piercing scream was almost deafening. Excited shouts mingled with her screams as the door rattled. It crashed open, just missing Moose as he jumped out of its way.

As the guards surged through the door, Ford slammed the teapot into the face of the first guard and felt a perverse sense of satisfaction as the man went down like stone.

At the same time, putting all his massive power behind the blows, Moose slammed the plates into the other guard's gut. The man doubled over, letting his rifle fly out of his hands.

Snatching it, Ford leveled it at the face of his guard. "Make a move and you're dead." He shifted the gun into Moose's hands. "I'm going after Olivia! You take care of these guys. And watch your back! Mujod could be anywhere."

"OLIVIA, listen to this inscription." Charlie had awakened after a catnap and his tired voice echoed through the chamber, drawing her to the wall where he sat. She knelt beside him, smiling despite the ache of fear eating her alive inside.

"'The gods who lived formerly rested in their pyramids. The beatified dead also, buried in their pyramids, and they who built houses, their places are no more.'" He ran his fingertips over each glyph as if to show her how the words were formed. "'I have heard the words of Imhotep and Hordedef. I have heard those songs that are in the ancient tombs and what they tell. The span of earthly things is as a dream. But a fair welcome is given him who has reached the west and the spell of our most powerful god.'"

"What does it mean?" she asked softly, staring at his chiseled profile.

"It's a magical incantation. Probably from the Middle Kingdom. This tomb is like a history lesson. Each wall has inscriptions dating from different time periods. It means this find, along with the Osiris puzzle box, will make me the hottest thing in archaeology for the next decade."

Olivia's heart skipped a beat. "That's providing we ever get out of here to tell the world about it."

"Of course we will." He struggled to sit up straighter. "I'm sorry. I should be trying to help you open the box, instead of showing off this incredible find. We need to plan how we can stall Mujod."

"Stalling won't be a problem. I've been studying and studying this miniature sarcophagus and I can't come up with a thing. I know this box has to open somehow." Fighting to stay calm, she resumed her position on the floor and picked up the box. She analyzed the casket, trying to find some sort of pattern, and her vision blurred into a prism of colors. She took a deep breath and shook her head. Maybe it was the stale air that made her eyes so tired.

Besides her, Charlie yawned. "Sorry, sis. I've been afraid to sleep for fear of what might happen. I'll move around to try to stay awake."

Fearful for his health, she shook her head and forced a laugh. "Go to sleep so I can concentrate. I'll wake you when I get it open."

His drowsy chuckle wasn't exactly reassuring. "Okay. Just for a minute." Almost before the echo of his words had died away, he gave in to exhaustion again.

She watched him, trying to gain strength from the fact that she had found him alive. The forces surrounding them were spinning out of control and she felt herself being caught up in them. She couldn't let that happen!

She gazed around the silent rock chamber. She'd never understood why Charlie had such a passion for spending his life in dark holes. She remembered the first time he'd taken her to the Institute in Chicago. He'd been so proud to show her the hermetically sealed room where they kept the mummies. Shivering, she could still see the pathetic figure of a woman, her skin blackened and shrunken, displayed in a clear glass case. She had wanted to wrap that poor creature in her linen shroud to spare her the indignity of being examined by strangers. Olivia had never forgotten that feeling. And she'd never again gone into that hermetically sealed room.

She shouldn't be shivering in the hot closed atmosphere, but she couldn't stop herself.

Suddenly, a hand touched her between her shoulder blades. She gasped and spun around. No one was there!

Charlie still lay across the room, curled in a fetal position on the granite floor.

No one had touched her, yet she couldn't shake the feeling that someone was very close by. Was she being watched?

The sensation became so strong, as if hands were on her body, she rose to her bare feet and backed slowly toward her brother's sleeping form. If she believed in ghosts, she'd think one or more of the poor souls who'd been buried alive in this mound haunted this place. Perhaps the power of their horror still vibrated through the ancient air.

Over a statue of Anubis, the representation of the eye of Horus drew her gaze. There was something almost otherworldly about it. She studied the drawing, the dark pupil surrounded by thick black lines, until her own eyes wouldn't focus anymore.

The eye moved.

She jumped, her pulse pounding through her veins so hard, her body shook.

"Charlie, wake up!" she gasped in terror.

In the corridor she could hear an ancient mechanism groan. Somehow, someone was opening the passageway!

Chapter Eleven

The burial mound might have been a natural formation to begin with, but man had changed it for his own use. That meant there was a doorway somewhere, maybe even two. Ford circled the rock face, trying to find some clue to where the entrance was hidden, pawing at every jutting formation. This architect had been ingenious; all the logical places denied him entrance.

If searching for Mujod over the barren desert had been bad, knowing Olivia was in this tomb and not being able to get to her was his worst nightmare.

Frantic, he stumbled around in the dark, cursing Mujod. When he got his hands on that bastard, he'd kill him for sure! Widening his circular path, he fell to his hands and knees to search the ground beside the mound.

He discovered the shaft by accident, tripping over it in his half-crazed scramble in the sand. He knew he was on the right track when he reached the first chamber and couldn't find the next doorway. The more complicated the location, the better the hiding place. If Mujod had found the damned entrance, then he sure could.

Ford had always considered his work a great adventure until this moment. Every delay scared the hell out of him. What was happening to Olivia? Were she and Charlie safe? Or had the cult already done something crazy?

He concentrated, trying to recall everything he'd ever studied about this particular type of mortuary temple. He remembered they were small-scale labyrinths, utilizing every trick the ancient Egyptians had ever learned to protect the sacred dead and their riches for the afterlife.

Stop thinking two-dimensionally.

He'd never figure out where that thought came from, but it was the answer. He bloodied his hands, scraping them across every inch of the walls. Finally, he jumped up to examine the surface of the wall above his reach.

That did the trick!

His throbbing hands caught on one projecting rock and then another. Handholds. He climbed as quickly as he could, closing his eyes and letting his sixth sense guide him to where the next would be.

This time the trapdoor mechanism was right where it should be. Nothing to it! The ceiling opened on command.

"Hang on, love, I'm coming." He murmured the words to himself over and over in the darkness like an ancient incantation. "Stay safe until I get to you."

Dizzy with success, Ford heaved himself into the passageway above. He was almost too big to make it, but panting and clawing, he found his way. A large block of granite barred the entry. This time he found the trick to the opening fairly quickly. Using a loose rock, he jammed the trapdoor open so he wouldn't get trapped, and more important, so Moose could follow him in.

DARKNESS CLOSED IN around Olivia and the floor beneath her feet felt unsteady. Someone was here, locked in the tomb with her and Charlie!

She couldn't give in to her fear. She would fight these madmen to the end.

"Charlie!" She called to him again, the sound echoing against stone over and over.

But he had fallen so deeply asleep that this time he didn't respond. Olivia felt trapped, frozen in a terror both psychological and physical. There was no out for her.

Whoever was outside this room, watching and waiting, was evil. She could feel his presence—knew he wanted to destroy her.

She shrank against Charlie's warm body, trying to convince herself that her imagination was working overtime. Whoever was out there was no more than a man—he might have superior height and weight, but he wasn't as clever as she.

Hearing a rustle beyond the walls, she looked around the tomb for some kind of weapon. She couldn't think anymore, all she could do was react.

She forced herself to leave Charlie and take backward steps toward the altar shelf. There was a foot-long ebony and gold sculpture of Anubis, a god with a jackal's head which, with its pointed ears, would make a great weapon. It weighed a ton. The thing must have been solid gold. With this in her hand she could knock any man out!

Steeling her courage, she took a position beside the opening. Whoever was coming would have to crawl in and she would be able to land a blow before he knew what was happening. With trembling arms she lifted the statue over her head and, her heart pumping like an engine, waited.

The person crept on, closer and closer. Terror beat in Olivia's pulse. She had to see the face of her enemy. Opening her eyes as wide as possible, she watched as the shadow in the small dark tunnel became a man.

"Ford!"

She drew a ragged breath of relief. He had found her! The statue went flying from her hand, hit the stone floor and rolled into a corner.

"Olivia!" He crushed her to his chest. "Are you all right, love?"

"Don't call me that!" She laughed and cried at the same time, the sting taken out of her words by the kisses she pressed all over his face.

"I'm fine." She sucked in as much air as possible to clear her head. "But Charlie's pretty bad. We have to get him out of here." She forced herself to let go of Ford and turn to her brother.

Cursing softly, Charlie was trying to pull himself upright. His eyes were nearly swollen shut with fatigue.

"You look like hell, Charlie. How do you feel?" Ford extended a steadying hand.

"Ford? You here?" He glanced around in surprise.

"Yes. We found you, you idiot. What the hell have you gotten yourself into?"

Charlie grinned. "Idiot, am I? I found it, Ford! In a cave on Bigeh! The Osiris box. It's over here. Let me show you."

He presented it to Ford as if it was something infinitely sacred. And perhaps to them it was. But now was the time to get away from this place. She couldn't explain it, but she knew evil still lurked nearby.

They exclaimed over the jeweled puzzle box as if it were the greatest discovery ever made. Adventure might be an integral part of the archaeologist's character but she found their disregard for danger absurd.

"Ford? Charlie...?"

They didn't seem to notice the new sound in the passageway. Maybe this was the evil she had sensed earlier. It wouldn't have been Ford coming to find her that had made her feel as though something terrifying hovered over her. She couldn't shake the feeling that someone else had been here before Ford arrived. Now it was coming back!

She raced to the corner, picked up the golden statue and shrank back against the wall to the doorway, prepared for anything.

Moose stuck his head through the opening. "Everything all right in here?"

Her knees sagged in relief and she dropped the statue to the floor again as Moose pulled Farita through the opening after him. The two continued holding hands even after they were safely in the chamber.

"You are safe!" Farita's happiness softened the lines of her face, her eyes a blur of tears.

After giving Olivia a rather startled look, Moose crossed to where Ford and Charlie stood savoring the box. "We must leave this place at once!"

Charlie didn't seem at all surprised to see Moose. He thrust the casket forward. "Look, Moose, I found it! The Osiris legend is true!" He slurred his words as if he were still half-asleep.

"Charlie, my friend, my heart is full that we find you alive and your quest successful. But now we must be very careful. I have immobilized two guards by handcuffing them to their car, but who knows how many more there are."

Ford glanced up. "What about Mujod?"

"He and the other guard were nowhere to be found. They must have fled into the desert."

"Foolish, Lieutenant Bey, to think I would depart without my treasure." Mujod stood in the entry, his lantern light gleaming off the rifle barrel in his hand. Another guard entered behind him and waved his gun to signify they should all huddle together in a corner.

The light wavered in the chamber, casting huge silhouettes on stone. It reminded Olivia of the shadow in the temple of Dendera and brought the same fear. Mujod must have been down here all along, waiting and watching. He was the evil she'd felt.

Ford held one of her hands in his. Glancing to her left, she saw Moose do the same with Farita. Behind them, Charlie clasped the treasure box in both hands.

"Do not try anything stupid, Dr. Harris," Mujod warned, pointing his gun straight at Ford's chest.

Something inside Olivia exploded. Ford would try anything to protect her. She had to keep him from doing something foolhardy. "Just take what you want and leave us alone!" she cried, rage pushing her to the edge.

He leered at her. "Miss Cranston, so brave and so vulnerable. That is precisely my plan. Farita, bring me the jeweled box!"

The guide looked dazed, her eyes dark pools in her pale face. She moved slowly to Charlie and held out her hand. But Charlie wouldn't turn over the box that easily.

Ford's eyes slitted. Only because she was watching him so closely did Olivia catch the signal he sent Moose. His grip remained the same on her hand, but she tensed, ready to do whatever was needed.

It was Moose who finally pried the box out of Charlie's fingers. "Here is what you want. Take it, Farita. Give it to Mujod."

She seemed puzzled by his attitude, but did as she was told. The box clutched in her hands, she took a step toward Mujod before turning to question Moose with a faint frown.

His eyes looked into hers, sending her some private communication that practically scorched the air around them. Tears ran down Farita's cheeks, making clean wet tracks on her dusty face as she reluctantly gave the box to Mujod.

"Betrayer." She spat at him in disgust.

He raised his hand to slap her, but seemed to think better of it when Moose looked ready to spring across the room.

Charlie's protesting groan went unheeded. Olivia knew exactly what the box meant to her brother and how he must feel to lose it. Involuntarily she moved toward him.

"Stay where you are, Miss Cranston!" Mujod snarled, losing his cool at last.

She stopped suddenly, realizing he meant to kill them. Now. He'd planned to all along. Who would ever find their bodies out here in this burial mound? Who would ever know?

"My humble apologies." His bow was a mockery. "Miss Cranston, please pick up the statue of Anubis and bring it here. I may as well take it all." Contempt curled his mouth as he looked at his former tour guide. "Help her, Farita! Anubis is solid gold and very heavy. We wouldn't want the precious Olivia hurt in any way."

"I hesitate to state the obvious, Mujod, but you can't get away with this. Interpol is already on your trail." Ford spoke as if he were making casual conversation. He wasn't frightened or intimidated—didn't he realize their lives were at stake?

She glanced over at him. Of course he did. He smiled at her, the way he had dozens of times before, as if they alone shared some fabulous secret.

"Do what he asks, Olivia. Give him the statue." Staring into his eyes, she caught his thoughts as clearly as if he spoke them.

Again, it took every ounce of her courage to march past the gunman, fully aware the light from the lantern revealed every curve of her body through the gauzy galabea. Farita stared at her for one long second before she knelt to help pick up the statue. She saw the idea planted by Moose taking form in the young woman's eyes, just as it had in hers when she looked at Ford. Olivia blinked to show Farita she understood.

"I'll take the head," Olivia said softly, cupping her hands around the statue's shoulders. "Be careful. This is very heavy."

Farita closed her hands around the base of the statue. Together, they stood and began moving toward the door.

"Mr. Mujod, the statue is so very heavy." Farita gasped and sagged to her knees, which knocked Olivia off balance. She, too, dropped to the stone floor.

"I'll get the damn thing!" Ford growled and stalked toward them.

"Stop!" Mujod waved his gun toward Olivia's breast.

Ford stopped dead. With a flick of his head, Mujod sent his henchman to retrieve the artifact. Olivia tensed as he stooped over her and muttered something in Arabic. She looked curiously at Farita for a translation.

"He wishes us to give him the statue," Farita told her slowly and distinctly, as if she were speaking to a child.

Olivia felt the subtle shift of the statue's weight in her hands and adjusted to it as Farita's grip tightened on her end. Unable to stop shaking, she gazed into the woman's dark eyes to gauge the right moment.

On cue, they swung the statue, hard, right below the guard's knees. Howling in pain, he tumbled backward. At the same moment, both Ford and Moose dived at Mujod, startling him into dropping his gun. Charlie, she wasn't surprised to see, went directly for the puzzle box.

A single shot rang out, echoing in the chamber, piercing Olivia's heart with fear. She picked up the statue of Anubis and held it in front of her like a club.

Ford stood over Mujod, who, writhing with pain, cupped one of his shoulders, blood oozing between his fingers. Framed in the entrance behind them, lit by a powerful beacon attached to her belt, stood Marta, the young South African woman from the tour.

Disbelief froze Olivia's feet to the floor. Marta stood as cool as could be, her cotton-candy hair frizzing, as usual. In her hand she held a small revolver. "I must say, you all managed very nicely, until I arrived." Her lazy smile altered slightly as she acknowledged Olivia's openmouthed shock. Of all the people on board the Emerald Empress, Marta would have been the last Olivia would peg for an Interpol agent.

"Interpol, I presume," Ford drawled. He peeled his shirt off and draped it over Olivia's shoulders, affording her some slight cover, leaving his arm around her protectively. "Where the hell have you been the last two weeks?"

"This operation has not gone precisely according to schedule." Marta's casual assessment made Olivia snuggle deeper into Ford's embrace. The admiring look the agent flashed at Ford's bare chest caused Olivia to think the most ungrateful thoughts, even if the woman had just rescued them. But Ford was right! Why hadn't the Interpol agent come forward earlier? A few minutes later and they might all have been dead!

Suddenly indignant at Marta's methodology, which had kept them all dangling dangerously, Olivia didn't feel so guilty. If she had screwed up their well-laid plans, they should have told her long before now!

"We have been on this one's trail for some time." Marta nudged Mujod's crumbled form with the toe of one shoe. "Besides his activities as a fence for stolen artifacts, we now have Miss Cranston's kidnapping to lay at his door."

"And mine!" Charlie roused himself enough to stagger over and check out this new arrival.

Suddenly, Han appeared in the entrance. "The area is secure, ma'am. I have two prisoners aboard the helicopter. Any orders, ma'am?" Gone was the solicitous father, replaced by an agent obeying orders from his superior.

Marta positively sparkled in her new role, appearing suddenly much older. "Radio for more backup. It appears we have an international incident on our hands."

For the first time, Olivia detected a slight accent in Marta's speech, although she still couldn't tell where the woman was really from. "We must get Charlie to a hospital. He's suffering from dehydration and malnutrition."

"Of course," Marta replied briskly.

"I must also accompany you." Farita stepped forward. "Although I was duped by Mr. Mujod, too, I fear it was I who took Olivia the drugged tea that made the kidnapping possible."

Marta glanced dispassionately around the group. "How many confessions are yet to come?"

"There *were* circumstances beyond her control. I shall go to police headquarters with her and testify to the help she has given us." Moose curled a protective hand around Farita's shoulder.

"There is room for everyone in the helicopter, but I do not think these treasures should be left unguarded. This looks to be a superb find, though this really isn't in my jurisdiction."

"I'll stay behind. Everything will need to be catalogued, packed properly and transported to Cairo," Ford volunteered, stepping away from Olivia.

She felt bereft, as if she were suddenly without support. There was a choice to be made. For the first time in her life, someone else had to come before Charlie.

"I'll stay, too."

Marta snorted. "I might have guessed." She turned toward Ford. "Your credentials are impeccable, Doctor. I will leave things in your capable hands. When we reach the helicopter, I'll radio ahead and send personnel to assist you."

Han reappeared and Marta nodded toward Mujod. "Take him. I shall follow with the others."

Only after the tour owner was hauled away did the gun disappear into the folds of Marta's split skirt. "Come. I must report in as soon as possible."

While Moose led Farita into the corridor, Olivia walked over to her brother. "Do you need any help?"

Although he was swaying on his feet, Charlie waved her away. "There will be plenty of help from Interpol. You must do what you think is right."

She gave him a hug, met the knowing glance from the eyes that were so like hers and smiled confidently. He understood, and that was all that mattered.

"I wouldn't leave the Osiris box with anyone but you." He put his treasure into her hand. "Ford is right. It will need to be examined properly in Cairo. You can trust him, you know."

Over the jeweled box, she smiled gently. "I know."

He grinned and gave her a playful jab, which turned into a gentle stroke. "I've seen Ford hang by one hand from the edge of a cliff just to copy an isolated inscription. It's going to be quite an adventure for the both of you. I envy you that." He gave her one quick tight hug that brought tears to her eyes. "I'll see you both in Luxor."

She held the box, so beautiful and mysterious, that had brought her to this place, and watched Marta shepherd Charlie, Farita and Moose from the tomb. When silence surrounded her, assuring she was alone with Ford, she turned to him. For a moment, time seemed suspended.

Then, slowly, he came to her. She realized she'd taken the first step down a new path. Could he sense it, too?

Together, they were on the brink of something entirely new and a bit terrifying.

Gently, he slid his hands around her throat, pushing his shirt off her shoulders. "I can't believe you stayed." He tilted her chin up with his thumbs. "There isn't enough time to tell you all I have to say."

For the first time, she opened herself to him, letting him see what she felt.

"I want to make love to you." His soft voice called to her. "There's nothing to be afraid of anymore. Without a leader, the cult won't be a threat to anyone."

She tilted her head back to gaze up at him longingly. "I don't want to make you any more conceited than you already are, but I have a confession. I'm not afraid of anything when I'm with you."

"Olivia!" He pulled her into his arms.

The jeweled box bit into her ribs and she pushed away, laughing. "Charlie's little reminder that our job's not quite done."

Ford let her go after a quick, hard kiss. His eyes narrowed with promise when he said, "There will come a time when nothing will interfere with what I have planned."

She caught her breath, her pulse already pounding at just the thought. Then he turned away to study the chamber, moving from inscription to inscription, all the while shaking his head.

"There's something not quite right here. I can't explain it, it's just a feeling, but in spite of the inscriptions, I think this might only be an antechamber. The real burial chamber for a mound this size should be larger. There should be some personal inscriptions. And if it has remained hidden for so long, there should be more treasure. Sit tight while I check a few ideas out."

Sit tight? Olivia sighed, resigned to the life she'd just chosen for herself. Ford was as single-minded as Charlie. She spread his shirt on the floor, brought the lantern that Marta had left and sat down cross-legged to reexamine Charlie's find.

Now that she wasn't under such terrible pressure, she could let her imagination take flight. It really was a beautiful piece of craftsmanship, with distinct figures following a pattern . . . Suddenly, she realized the artist had been telling a story.

The more she stared at the jewels and gold inlay, the more certain she became. She glanced around to ask Ford a question but he was running his hands over the far wall and muttering incomprehensibly. She returned her attention to the puzzle box. The lapis pieces were repeated over and over again. She stood the box upright and squinted at it, trying to form a general impression. The pieces reformed in her mind into a woman carrying something gold in her hands. The carnelian represented another figure. Perhaps a man?

"I'll be be right back." Ford startled her by pressing a kiss on the top of her head. "I want to check some dimensions in the corridor."

She watched him go, fighting her sudden feeling of panic. This was what archaeologists did. She'd better start getting used to it right now.

He shuffled and scuffed around the doorway, whistling softly to himself. His noises were strangely reassuring—she didn't want to be left alone in this place for a second!

Concentrating, she again followed the design with her fingers and tried to make sense of the story. She closed her eyes, designing a tapestry. What did she know of the legend? Could the artist have been recreating a part of the Isis-Osiris story?

In her mind the representations began to change shape, matching the forms of lapis and carnelian on the box. The lapis woman pressed a gold piece into the carnelian man's chest. He fell to his knees and she appeared behind him. He stood and bent over her, kissing her mouth. Carnelian and lapis then merged into one and disappeared. Then the pattern was repeated.

She opened her eyes and found she'd been unconsciously turning the puzzle box in her hands. She'd been around the box one revolution. But had she started at the right place?

She closed her eyes, running the scenes together in her mind as if they were a movie. Her heart began thudding in her chest. She could hardly breathe. Could she . . . ? Had she . . . ?

She turned the box around again, pressing on the gold piece everywhere it appeared in the lapis hands.

Slowly the lid slid open.

She gasped in stunned disbelief as she stared down into the casket. All along, Charlie had said the box contained the left hand of Osiris; but, until this moment, she hadn't really believed him.

There, nestled in a linen wrap, was a golden hand. It was so exquisite, tears come to Olivia's eyes. She could almost feel the pain of the goddess, Isis, lamenting the loss of her love, Osiris.

Strangely enough, she couldn't permit herself to touch the treasure, much less remove it from its resting place. She couldn't stop an enormous wave of sadness and guilt from washing over her.

Was she any better than the grave robbers of old?

Footsteps sounded behind her. Ford must have come back into the room while she was concentrating. She looked up to share this triumph with him.

Olivia's smile suddenly faded and she blinked in confusion.

A shadow was reflected on the walls all around her. It wasn't Ford, but a giant Osiris, his arms stretched out in front of him. For a moment, she didn't believe her eyes. Then the shadow, wearing his distinct but oddly shaped crown, began to move slowly toward her.

Chapter Twelve

She couldn't move. She couldn't speak. She couldn't think. For the first time in her life, Olivia knew what total terror was. It was living a nightmare—not knowing what was real and what might be a frightening figment of her imagination.

She tried to scream for Ford, but she couldn't make her lips work. The apparition drew closer. Somehow she caught a thread of sanity and clung to it. This was no ghost of the great Osiris, brought back by her solving the riddle of the puzzle box. This was simply a man dressed as an ancient Egyptian, wearing a false beard on his chin and the white crown of Upper Egypt on his head.

She stood to face him, clutching the puzzle box, still open, to her breast. Digging her bare toes into Ford's shirt and bunching her thigh muscles, she prepared to run. But at the precise moment she was to make her escape, the apparition turned into a mere mortal and her knees buckled in response.

"Akim!"

His eyes glittered wildly, gazing right through her as if he didn't recognize her. He seemed to be in a trance or under the influence of a hypnotic drug. "Isis, goddess and great enchantress, I greet you. To breathe the breath of Isis is to make passage to heaven. The span of earthly things is as a dream."

"Akim..." She paused to swallow her terror. Just a man, she reminded herself. And a nice man, if she could get through to him. She cleared her throat. "Under Secretary Tamarin, where is Dr. Harris?"

He smiled, an oddly distant smile that ripped the fragile thread of reality out of her grasp. He was too far gone for her to reach.

"My friend, Ford, has fulfilled his destiny. He has found the treasure of a lifetime. We must join him, my beautiful queen. But first, you must prepare yourself."

Only then did she notice the gauzy material he held in his hands. The wild glint in his eyes made her take a deep breath before she asked, "Where is Ford?"

"First you must prepare yourself." He repeated the words like a chant. "Isis. Goddess. Lady with words of power." He thrust the fabric at her with an odd little jerky motion that was at the same time almost reverent. "You must put these on to perform magic."

Where was Ford? Couldn't he hear or see what was happening?

For one horrifying instant, she wondered if he might have put the find of a lifetime before her. No! Ford would never leave her to this!

Relentlessly Akim stalked her, forcing her out of the chamber and into the passageway. "Do not doubt me, Isis. I have taken Ford to my secret place."

The "secret place" must be what Ford was searching for—the real burial vault. She didn't dare look away from Akim's eyes, but she backed steadily away from him, farther and farther from the light. She had no idea how far this passage went, she only knew she must stay out of Akim's reach.

"Ford." She hissed his name and when there was no reaction from the man in front of her, she dared to call again, louder. "Ford!" Her answer was silence.

Akim threw her a look of pity. "You will see your Ford only when you are properly attired."

At last she realized there was no one to rescue her. In desperation she stopped in a corridor parallel to the entryway. "All right, Under Secretary Tamarin. What do you wish me to do?" She took from his hands some of the finest linen she'd ever seen.

"This is your ancient raiment, goddess, lovingly preserved so you may fulfill your role as Isis."

She looked with horror from the sheer fabric into Akim's face and pulled her galabea protectively around her body. "But it's see-through."

"Here at the waist is a narrow strip which is knotted around the figure to keep the garment in position," he continued as if she hadn't spoken.

"Where's Ford?" She was at the end of her patience and strength. This had to be a nightmare. She took a deep breath, willing herself to wake up.

Tilting his head, Akim blinked. His eyes cleared, and for the first time he really looked at her. "I will take you to him, Olivia. But first you must be properly attired."

This was no dream. Shaking so badly her teeth chattered, she stepped deeper into the shadows and turned her back. She laid the jeweled casket at her feet, then slid the bottom half of the linen square up under the galabea, wrapping it around her bare waist. It was almost impossible to raise the galabea from her shoulders and let it slide down to a pool around her feet.

She felt Akim's eyes burn into her nudity and hurriedly draped the linen across her chest, not knowing exactly how to arrange it.

"The cape must be draped across your shoulders and the corners twisted in your hands until they become cords. Then they are knotted across your breasts." Akim's fingers brushed her bare breast.

She shrieked in revulsion and backed away two steps, hastily wrapping the fabric around her, making a clumsy knot at her waist. Then she scooped up the casket and held it in front of her exposed body, using it as a small shield.

"I've done what you wanted. Now take me to Ford!"

His eyes dropped to the puzzle box and widened in approval. "Only Isis, my consort, could have performed such great magic." Suddenly, his hard hand closed over her forearm and pulled her toward him. "At last the time has come."

The cruel grip of his hand and the insane note in his voice should have made her fight him with her teeth, her nails—anything to get away. Instead, she allowed him to pull her down the passageway. He would take her to Ford. That was all that mattered now.

Akim stopped in the darkness, and, as if he had performed this ritual many times, swept his free hand over the inscriptions in a weaving pattern. Then he pushed against solid rock.

The tunnel he revealed sloped downward at a steep angle, down into blackness. The opening couldn't have been more than three feet high and two feet wide. Loose stones covered the floor as if all the weight of the rock above had slowly, inevitably, begun to disintegrate.

He motioned her in and she bent nearly double to fit. There was no light at all, only his fingers prodding her forward. Dread made the journey a nightmare. Only Akim's hot breath at her back kept her moving forward with any semblance of control. That and the need to find Ford.

Then a soft glow appeared ahead. Olivia began to run, anxious to get out of the confining space, desperate to find Ford.

She entered a huge chamber with a fifteen-to-twenty-foot ceiling. Oil lamps were placed on the floor at regular intervals, completely illuminating the interior. Wild with fear, she glanced around, barely noting the riches piled everywhere, the magnificent colors on the walls.

She was only interested in one thing.

"Where is Ford?" She whirled to face Akim, her fingers still clasping the forgotten puzzle box.

"He is there, beneath the stela."

At first she thought him part of the decoration, the dim light casting his profile in gold as he lay, his wrists and ankles bound by linen strips, stretched out on an elaborate ceremonial stone slab.

"Oh, God, no!" She ran to him, collapsing before the shrine, tears choking her.

Placing the puzzle box beside him, she laid her cheek on his chest above his heart. The steady beat reassured her and brought tears of joy to her eyes. "Oh, you're alive!"

A sob caught in her throat. "You're going to be all right, love, I promise." Smearing his face and throat with wet kisses, Olivia tried to revive him. "Wake up, Ford. I need you."

His eyes remained closed. Beneath his tan he looked deathly pale. "Ford, love, please wake up." She brushed his hair off his forehead and her searching fingers found a patch of dried blood. She turned to Akim angrily. "What have you done to him?"

"The doctor is merely stunned. I could not have him learn of the entryway. Do not look so distressed, my enchantress. You know the stela is a talisman of invincible power to heal him." Akim approached the foot of the slab where Ford lay. There, balanced on a convex base, stood a striking stone tablet. Its top, sides and base were covered with hieroglyphics.

She'd never seen anything like it before. It was beautiful, and yet the way Akim stared at it frightened her.

"It has been so long, my queen. But surely you remember! Ra gave you the words of power that enabled you to raise me from the dead." Akim moved toward her holding out his palm. "My lovely Isis. If not for you, I would have been lost for eternity. But you gathered me up and recited the incantations of irresistible might."

Making the only decision she could, she stepped toward him, placing her hand on his. Maybe if she went along with this craziness, she could keep him calm and buy time.

He drew her away from Ford, out into the center of the room. His hands swung in a wide arc, as if to show her the scope of the surrounding riches, then he turned, sliding his hands caressingly over her shoulders and down her bare arms to link their fingers. "A knowledge of the gods and of the magical texts of the stela makes us masters of all the powers of heaven, earth and the underworld."

Paralyzed by the dementia she saw in his eyes, Olivia stared at him. "What do you want from me?" she finally gasped through her tight dry throat.

"I have waited so long for you, my Isis." He lifted her captured fingers and slowly rotated their joined hands across the tips of her breasts.

She shrank from his touch. "You're crazy, Akim! I'm not Isis, any more than you're Osiris!"

He appeared not to hear her but held her even more tightly, seemingly mesmerized by the movements of their joined hands across her breasts, down her stomach, rubbing back and forth at the apex of her thighs.

Nausea burned at the back of her throat, but she held herself rigid, afraid that any slight movement would send him totally over the edge.

"For more than twenty-five hundred years, since the days of Herodotus, we have waited for you to return."

His irrational words reinforced her resolve to block out the feel of his hands caressing her body. This madman wasn't touching her but an imaginary goddess. If she could only find a way to get her and Ford out of this nightmare...

Like a lover, he lifted her trapped hands over her head so her body involuntarily arched toward his.

"We two are the only beings who live in a netherworld of our own choosing. We possess irrational powers and menaces. We, alone, have the power to move men's thoughts."

Suddenly, Olivia couldn't stand it another second. If Akim didn't take his hands off her body, she would start screaming and never stop.

She pulled free and twisted away to look at Ford. He remained motionless, helpless, vulnerable. It was up to her now. She began to tremble and hated herself for her vulnerability. Anything, anything would be better than feeling so helpless. She forced herself to turn back to Akim.

"What do you wish me to do?" she asked quietly.

"Perform your magic!" At last he released her and she backed to the edge of Ford's bier, using it for support.

"I have gathered all the amulets for the ceremony." He disappeared into an antechamber.

Collapsing in relief, she threw her arms around Ford's body. "Please, love, wake up! Please!" She pressed a kiss on his cool lips, hoping for a miracle.

When there was none, she dragged herself away from him. Surely somewhere in this room she would find a weapon to use against Akim.

From what little she'd learned, she recognized the room was filled with priceless relics. There was a canopy bed, a carrying chair and armchairs of wood with thin sheets of ebony veneer more beautiful than any furniture she'd ever seen. Hieroglyphics inlaid in gold on the ebony background were carved in such detail that every feather of the tiny birds and every scale of the little serpents was clearly distinct.

Six alabaster jars sat along one wall. They were too heavy for her purpose. She wondered what they had held, for their seals were all broken and she couldn't detect anything inside.

Several mummy cases, looking so brightly beautiful that they could have been brand-new, rested on a stone bed like the one where Ford lay. She had started toward them, hoping to find a piece of gold just heavy enough to knock Akim out when he appeared before her, carrying the carnelian thet amulet she'd seen Ford steal from the museum what seemed a lifetime ago.

But Akim hardly seemed to notice she was there. He walked directly past her without saying a word, went around the bier and dropped the amulet into a golden vessel filled with water, crushing some strange flower over it. Then he turned around and disappeared again.

She had to take advantage of every second! She rushed to a chest overflowing with jewelry and small items she didn't recognize. She needed to find a weapon—anything that might stop him!

She whirled again as Akim appeared, carrying the gold statue of Ament. With great reverence, he placed it next to the stela.

"One last talisman and we shall begin," he announced to the room, never looking at her.

Desperation burned at her insides. She rushed to Ford and rubbed her hands up and down his bare chest, trying to revive him.

"Ford, please! Wake up!"

As if he had heard her, he groaned, low in his chest.

"Thank God!" Sobbing in relief, she fumbled with the linen strips wound around his wrists, trying to free him.

"Here are the writings you must have for your magic." Akim dragged a stone tablet into the center of the chamber.

Remembering Charlie's notes and what Ford had told her, she knew this must be the tablet from the Book of the Dead that had been stolen from the museum.

Olivia stood in front of Ford, blocking Akim's view. With one hand behind her, she kept picking away at his bindings.

Akim's dark expressive eyes were wildly intense as he stared at her. "Now, Isis, use the words of power! Use your knowledge to pronounce them so all the gods of heaven, earth and beyond will be compelled to listen and obliged to fulfill your behest."

He walked toward her, his hands outstretched pleadingly. "The time of the ceremony is upon us."

Olivia shrank back across Ford's body as much to protect him as to draw strength. Akim lifted his hand, beckoning her toward the stela.

She remained standing where she was, close to Ford, some remnant of her old spirit sparking to life inside her. "I will do what you wish. But *first* you must perform a service for me."

For an instant, surprise flickered in Akim's eyes. At last, a rational emotion she recognized and could deal with!

"You must grant my request or I won't be able to grant yours."

He bowed and his stiffly curled false beard hit his chest. "How may I serve you, great Isis?"

"There is an unbeliever present. I cannot perform my magic unless he is gone. You must send Ford safely away from this place at once. Only then will I use my magic words of power."

"YOU MUST SEND Ford safely away from this place at once. Only then will I use my magic words of power."

Ford heard the words but they made no sense to him. He tried to sit up and groaned, reaching for the pain knifing through his head and finding, to his great amazement, that his hands were bound together.

"I'm not going anywhere without you." He didn't know if the words he muttered made any sense, he only knew they were true.

Using his elbows, he pushed himself up, and found himself leaning heavily against Olivia's back. After all this time, her exotic scent still clung to her. It wrapped around him, comforting him.

What the hell had happened?

Prying his eyes open despite his crashing headache, he blinked in disbelief. They were in a chamber filled with riches as fabulous as those found in Tut's tomb. And the wall paintings were magnificent. The find of a lifetime!

Maybe he was dreaming. Why else would Olivia be dressed in an impossibly provocative drape and Akim be standing in the center of the chamber dressed as Osiris?

"What in hell is going on here?" he roared, feeling Olivia tremble against him. "What is this all about, Akim?"

The dark eyes flickered with a spark of recognition, then all sanity vanished. Akim reached into the jewelry chest and pulled out the crook and the flail to cross over his chest. Staring at Olivia, he quivered impatiently, his false beard jutting forward. "There is no time to explain. The ceremony must begin now!"

"What damn ceremony are you talking about? Untie me, damn it!" He rose to his feet and tried to take a step. Instead, he tumbled forward and crashed to the floor.

Olivia's tear-stained face hovered over him in mute appeal. "Ford, Akim and I must perform our magic now. You have to leave. Release him so he can go, Akim."

His heart stopped as he realized how much she was willing to sacrifice for his sake. He sat bolt upright, his hands clenched into fists. "Akim, I'm an archaeologist first. I can't leave until I know how you discovered this site and why it's been kept secret from the world."

If he could keep Akim off-balance, make him answer some questions, maybe he could bring him back to sanity. Marta had said she would send backup. He just had to keep Akim occupied until then. He noticed the linen strips around his wrists were looser than those binding his ankles. That was a beginning.

"Of course you are consumed with curiosity. It is to be expected. Allow me to ease you back against your bed of stone, where you belong."

"No! Don't touch him!" Olivia snarled, her eyes shooting flames. She threw herself across his body to protect him.

Ford had lusted after her the instant he'd laid eyes on her. Now he ached inside with love for her. He would never forget this moment. It burned into his soul. He vowed to spend the rest of his life showing Olivia how much she meant to him.

"Please, allow me to make my friend more comfortable for the short time he will be with us." Akim sounded solicitous and his hands were gentle as they eased Ford back against the stone slab, but Olivia stayed right at his side, ready to spring to his defense at the slightest hint of danger.

Any vestige of sanity Akim still possessed was buried so deep, it would never stand up against this crazy obsession. But what had caused him to lose his senses?

Ford had to know, and to find out he had to keep Akim talking. Under the cover of her skimpy dress, he felt Olivia's fingers working at the linen strips around his hands.

"Akim, for our friendship, explain this place," he urged.

"Look around you!" Akim rose to his feet, a certain pagan majesty in the way he flung his arms out to embrace the riches piled around the stone chamber. "My ancestors discovered it generations ago. Archaeologists from around the world were plundering our treasures, sending them away from our land, so they kept it quiet. Later, by which time it might have been safer to share our secret, this place had seeped into our souls. My grandfather and his before him and his before him studied the old ways. They worshiped the ancient gods. I thought them foolish old men. Then eighteen months ago, I realized the old magic must be evoked."

A terrible sadness stamped Akim's face with such pain, Ford knew at once what had ripped away the man's sanity. Leda, his wife, had died giving birth to a son eighteen months ago.

"You began stealing artifacts then, didn't you?" Ford was grasping at straws, anything to keep Akim talking. He could feel Olivia's fingers working frantically. Her bravery made him feel invincible. Somehow, together, they'd survive this new trial.

"All of this—the amulet, the goddess statue, the puzzle box and the magical texts of the Book of the Dead—they are all for the resurrection ceremony?" Ford stopped but there was no answer.

"Are they, Akim?" he insisted, burning with compassion for his friend, so alone, so lost. He hesitated a moment, then said, "But you must know, nothing will bring them back to you."

"Isis *can* and *will.*" In one swift movement, Akim grabbed Olivia, tearing her from Ford's side.

She screamed and Akim clamped his hand over her mouth. Trying to lunge forward, Ford fell again, helpless. He cursed himself for not sending Olivia to safety with the others. He had wanted her to stay. He had been selfish, and now they would both pay the price.

And he cursed Akim, mad with grief, who held Olivia tightly against him.

"Let her go, Akim!" he shouted, fighting his bonds, fighting the frustration ripping him apart. "Let Olivia go."

"She is Isis, returned to do my bidding. She opened the box. Only Isis could work such magic."

He spared a glance for the puzzle box lying open beside him and gasped at the perfection of the beautiful gold hand resting in the casket.

"You see. She has the power! These are the words that tell how Isis bestowed upon the deceased her magical powers of life. I have steeped the thet amulet in the water of the ankhami flower. Now only one thing remains."

He dragged Olivia, protesting, to one of the mummy cases lining the wall. Frantically, Ford worked at his bonds. Sweat poured down his body, soaking the linen, tightening it even more around his fingers.

"Akim, stop!" he shouted. "Olivia, don't look!"

Seemingly oblivious to Ford, Akim held Olivia with one hand and with the other lifted the lid to one of the mummy cases.

Olivia's scream ripped through Ford's body and her eyes widened in horror. Resting in the chest were the wrapped bodies of a woman and an infant.

Akim turned to gaze at Ford with a kind of pride. "I performed the ritual here, in this very place. I had studied the old ways like my father, so I knew what to do. I removed their internal organs and placed them in canopic jars." He flung open a small square chest where eight carved alabaster jars were placed together. Four large and four small.

Olivia flung her hand over her mouth, fighting not to be sick. She struggled in Akim's iron grip, but couldn't break free. At that moment, Ford knew that having come this far, nothing would stop Akim now.

"Are they not beautiful, Ford? Fitting for my wife and son."

Tears washed over Akim's hand as Olivia wept. Pity replaced horror in her eyes.

Ford groaned in anguish at Akim's mad grief and raged against the bonds making him helpless. "Akim, let me help you."

"Thank you, my friend, but I have done all that is necessary." He smiled, as if his actions had been perfectly normal. "I cleaned and anointed their empty bodies, then filled their abdomens with the finest linen. Finally, I washed and treated their flesh with precious ointment before wrapping them. It took a long time to accomplish, but now, their wait is over."

He reached out and placed the thet amulet on the neck of his dead wife. Releasing Olivia, he demanded, "Now, say the words."

Anguished, Olivia turned to meet Ford's eyes. Lifting her head like the queen Akim thought her to be, she slowly turned to face him. "I'm so very sorry. I can't."

"Say the words!" The scream of pain came from Akim's sick soul.

"I don't know the words, Akim. No one does." Carefully, she backed away from him.

Akim turned on her, grief intensifying the anger in his eyes. He spread his arms like a bird of prey and darted after her.

"Akim, wait! I have an idea!" Ford shouted, trying to draw his attention away from Olivia. He clawed at his bonds, feeling the sting of his sweat dripping into his cuts and mingling with warm blood.

Reaching Olivia, Akim grabbed her by the hair. He pulled her toward the casket with one hand while the other slipped into the folds of his skirt and pulled out a long razor-sharp knife.

"No!" Ford fought his bindings, knocking the puzzle box on its side. The beautiful gold hand came out of the box and seemed to open. Or maybe it was only a trick of the light.

"Run, Olivia!" he bellowed, trying to hurl his body across the floor to get to her.

Akim trapped her between himself and the mummy case and bent her back over the bodies of his dead wife and child. He raised the knife over her and she screamed.

"Let the blood of Isis and the magical powers of Isis and the words of power of Isis be mighty enough to protect and keep you safely, Leda and my son."

The chant rang through the chamber, mingling with Olivia's screams.

The hair rose on the back of Ford's arms. At last he forced one hand free and snatched the nearest object within reach. As the knife plunged toward Olivia's exposed throat, Ford threw the golden hand of Osiris with all his might.

Chapter Thirteen

The golden hand blurred with the knife blade into one bright flash and together they spun off into the shadows. Akim froze, looking confused, seemingly unable to comprehend the disintegration of all his plans. In that moment, Ford bent down, pulled the bindings from his ankles and launched himself forward, wrestling Akim away from Olivia.

The sounds of grunts and gasps, and the thud of bodies smashing into jars and chests, knocking over the beautiful furniture and extinguishing some of the lamps, echoed over and over in the stone chamber.

If she was going to help Ford, she had to find the knife! Olivia scrambled to the corner on her hands and knees, feeling around in the darkness. Finally, she saw a glint of metal to her left. She reached for it.

It was the golden hand. She turned it over and amazement pounded through her. What she thought was solid gold had only been a cover! It was open, revealing a perfect hiding place. Where there had been one hand, now there were two.

Inside the golden hand lay a mummified hand, black, withered and dry. Was *this* the hand of Osiris?

Had the legend been so focused on eternal life and Isis's devotion that it had missed the truth? Or had that long-ago queen decided to hide reality from those who might destroy it?

A wave of pity and regret washed over her. Whoever had buried this had done it with great love and devotion. Now, thousands of years later, it was exposed, vulnerable to speculation and testing. It seemed almost blasphemous to her.

Behind her the scuffling stopped. She turned, curiously calm. Akim lay half-sitting, half-sprawling against the large case that held his wife and child. His eyes were closed and blood spilled from his broken nose. Standing over him, legs braced wide apart, fists clenched at his sides, Ford resembled a vengeful god.

He turned to her, light blazing in his eyes. Slowly, his expression changed, softened, and a moment later he enfolded her in his arms. She pressed herself against him, needing to hold on to him, to glory in being alive and together.

"Love, are you all right?" His lips trailed down her throat and back to her mouth. She opened herself to his sweet deep kisses, allowing him to feel her vulnerability. Never had she wanted to give herself to anyone so completely.

Ford cupped her face, his fingers caressing her cheeks. "Did he hurt you?"

Shaking her head, she pressed her lips into one of his bleeding palms. "Look what was inside the gold hand," she whispered.

She pushed the artifact toward him. As it moved, the mummified hand came out of its golden casket, falling into Ford's flesh-and-blood hand. It looked small and pathetic against his vibrant skin.

"Could the legend be true? Could this really be the hand of Osiris?" His low voice contained an archaeologist's thirst for knowledge.

"Is there any way to prove that?" An idea that would horrify her twin sprang into her head.

"We could carbon-date it, but we could never positively link it to any specific individual. The only way we do that is if we find an intact mummy in the sarcophagus. Like Tut." He turned the hand over gently. "There's something else here. I can tell by the weight."

Picking at the wrapping, ever so carefully, he exposed a heavy gold ring, not on any of the fingers, but resting against the palm. It was a large scarab—the symbol of eternal renewal—fashioned out of precious gems exquisitely set in gold.

"Charlie may have found the box, but you, my love, have found the prize. We'll be able to tell by the workmanship on the ring if it comes from the Old or Middle Kingdom," he said.

She grabbed his upper arm. "Then let's date the ring. We'll tell everyone it was inside the golden hand." Determined to make her point, she tilted her head back to look him square in the eyes. "Once this person lived and breathed like us. He loved and was loved in return. He deserves the dignity of resting in peace." She paused before making her plea. "I want to take this mummified hand out into the desert, where it belongs, and bury it."

Ford stared at her intently. "Olivia, I can't..."

Holding nothing back, she let him see right into her soul.

"I must be demented," he breathed. "Okay. Let's do it. Now, before I come to my senses!"

She began to tremble, not with fear, but with love for him. As of this moment, everything changed. Forever. A lifetime wouldn't be long enough to touch Ford, to know him, to love him.

"Thank you." Sighing, she leaned her face against his shoulder.

Something flashed behind Ford's back. Olivia screamed and he spun around, ready to defend her. But no defense was necessary.

Akim had somehow managed to pull himself up and was trying to climb into the chest with his wife and child's mummies. Ford raced toward him, but before he could reach the mummy case, Akim had slammed the lid shut, locking himself in.

Ford pushed at the top, all the muscles in his arms, across his chest and back bunching and rippling with the exertion.

"Get me something to pry this thing open!" he shouted over his shoulder. "He'll suffocate in there if we don't get him out soon!"

Olivia spotted Akim's knife in a corner and took it to Ford. "Here, see if this works. Maybe there's some design on this box I can figure out that will open it."

She looped up one end of her linen skirt and wound it around her waist. Into the makeshift pocket she placed the mummified hand, the golden hand and the ring. Then, on her hands and knees, she studied the long box, trying to decipher a pattern. All the time,

Ford kept calling Akim's name, urging him to open the lid.

Olivia crept around the mummy case, shaken by what she'd just witnessed. How could Akim be so desperate? Then she looked at Ford and realized, if she lost him, she would also feel as though she'd lost everything.

The floor moved under her palms.

Olivia stood up just as another tremor hit, growling up from the center of the earth. The statue of Ament fell, rolling across the floor. She heard glass breaking in the darkness as lamps toppled over. She tried to grab on to something solid and could find nothing. Suddenly, a huge fragment of stone cracked off the ceiling and dropped onto the stela, crushing it completely.

"It's an aftershock! Get out of here, Olivia!" Ford shouted at her while frantically clawing at the lid of the mummy case. "Go! Now!"

Another tremor flung her back to her knees, and her scream was lost in the thunderous crash of splitting stones. The ceiling rumbled above them, a trickle of small stones falling over the case Ford fought to open. A menacing low rumble started in the granite all around them.

"Get out of here, Olivia!"

"I won't go without you," she said, sobbing, pulling at his arm. Tears streamed down her cheeks, more sobs of anguish building up behind a dam of pain in her chest, but she held on to him. "I won't go without you!" she repeated.

Every irrational fear she'd felt about the tons of stone and earth bearing down on her broke free, pouring through her. Using a strength born out of that terror, she yanked Ford away from the mummy case. They fell and the earth shook again, sending them rolling across the floor as tons of rock fell straight down, covering the mummy case and everything around it.

"Let's get out of here!" She grabbed his hand with iron fingers, dragging him toward the tunnel.

"Wait! I see the puzzle box. Let me get that for Charlie." He turned to go toward the bier as the side walls began to crack.

She couldn't breathe or see anything with all the dust in the air. Where was he? They had to get out of the burial mound, if it was still possible—there were so many passages and rooms between them and the outside.

She felt his arms wrap around her, his body protecting her, propelling her toward safety. They emerged into the passageway in a blast of dust and tiny rock particles that stung her skin. Behind them the doorway filled with rubble.

Ford went first, pulling her forward. She kept one hand cradled around the makeshift pocket, determined that she wouldn't lose the treasure they had suffered so much for.

They had to crawl through to the second chamber. Stephen Phipps waited there, a gun in his hand.

She froze in stunned disbelief, too tired and frightened to protest when Ford shoved her from him. His muscles bunched in an adrenaline rush.

"Bloody hell, where the devil have you been hiding? I've been searching this whole bloody maze for half an hour." Lifting one eyebrow, Stephen gave them a cheeky grin. "Surprise you, did I? Marta sent me ahead of the rest of the team. Someone from your institute is on the way, Dr. Harris."

"You and Marta are both from Interpol?" Weakly, Olivia stepped toward Ford, anxious for the protective curve of his arm. "I thought the two of you were having a fling."

"With that barracuda!" Chuckling, he slid his gun into a shoulder holster. "The likes of her would take this Manchester lad and toy with him like a tabby with a mouse. Bloody fine agent, though."

He glanced uneasily at the ceiling as the ground rumbled again. "There! That was a nasty one. We better get moving. Where are the stolen artifacts and the relics Marta ordered me to guard?"

"Buried deep within Egyptian soil." Ford glanced down, seeming surprised that he still held the puzzle box in one hand. "All except this."

Pushing her hand into her skirt loop, Olivia carefully separated the mummy hand. "And these." The ring had tumbled into the golden hand, which had closed partially around it.

The gold glittered on her filthy palm as Stephen whistled, impressed.

"This is all we could salvage when the chamber collapsed." Ford spoke quietly, his slight smile for their very private secret.

"Bloody beautiful, I'm sure." Shuddering, Stephen glanced around as they dropped into the first chamber. "If this is the sort of place you archaeologists spend time in, I'm happy to be an agent. Place gives me the quivers."

"There's no need for you to be down here to guard anything now. It will take us a decade to retrieve the contents of that burial chamber, if it all isn't smashed to pieces."

Ford was silent as he led the way out of the labyrinth that had very nearly been their tomb. The earth had been silent now for the last ten minutes. Bathed in moonlight, the barren landscape looked serenely beautiful.

Below, in the caverns, she'd lost all track of time and of reality. She was finding it all too hard to believe.

Stephen ran to a Land Rover parked nearby and checked in by radio. "Aftershocks are all finished. No further damage reported," he announced to them when he returned.

"Good. You can wait for the others. Olivia and I just want to get the hell away from here. If anyone asks, we're heading to the Doclea Oasis."

Ford grabbed her hand, but she resisted for a moment. "Was *anyone* on board the Empress who they were supposed to be?" she asked Stephen.

"Those nice ladies from the States." Shrugging, he glanced at Ford. "Marta's team was assigned to Dr. Harris from the minute he contacted us. I've been working on Ray for months. When everyone booked passage on the Emerald Empress, we knew we were on to something. My aunt Irmie has been trailing you since you arrived at the Cairo airport. We had a hard time with you blundering into our operation."

So that's who she had felt following her! Swaying back against Ford's bare chest, Olivia felt his arms wrap protectively around her. Only then did she remember the thin linen shielding her body. A hot blush heated her skin, but she had one more question to ask.

"Is she really your aunt?"

"Bloody right! She taught me everything I know about the spy business!" he crowed with pride.

Chuckling, Ford pressed a kiss to the side of her neck. "Satisfied?" He looked at Stephen. "Okay if I borrow your Land Rover?" Without really waiting for an answer, he pulled Olivia toward the car. As they drove away a helicopter was already overhead.

Ford drove seemingly without a plan, deep into the landscape of weirdly eroded sandstone and vast desert. The farther they got from the mound, the more profound the peace of the dark night became.

There was just the two of them, alone in a vast wilderness. Olivia searched his profile, etched by moonlight as he stared straight ahead. She tried to think of something to say. Was he upset? Did he regret bringing the hand away with them? She patted it gently through her thin skirt. She would never regret her decision. It was the right thing to do.

Twenty minutes later, he pulled the vehicle to a stop in the middle of nowhere. She looked around. There were no markers to guide her. She would never to be able to find this place again.

"We'll bury it here." He walked to the back of the car and searched through the equipment. "All Land Rovers come equipped with shovels in case the driver gets caught in a sandstorm and has to dig himself out."

"Ford?" She waited until he looked at her. "Why here?"

"Because I don't know where we are. I've been zig-zagging the whole way. And *he* should be safe here."

He walked to a slight depression and began digging. Before long he hit a rock. Carefully edging around it, he struggled to lift it sideways. Then he created a shallow grave. He looked up at her, his face stern and beautiful in the unearthly moonlight.

"Do it."

Instinct told her she had to do this on his terms. Without ceremony, she tugged at her linen skirt until she ripped a fragment free. She used it as a shroud for the hand. She didn't know any ancient incantations or Egyptian prayers, so she silently hoped whoever the hand belonged to and whoever had buried it so carefully would now rest peacefully.

She stepped away as Ford threw a shovelful of sand over the hand and then replaced the rock, tamping it down. He shovelled more sand on top of it until all trace that they had ever dug there disappeared. The hand was finally returned to the earth.

"Bodies laid in the Egyptian sand need no other means of preservation than the heat and dryness. It will stay there for eternity. Does that please you, Olivia?"

She looked at him, her eyes filled with love, and he kissed her.

HE COULDN'T STOP himself from sliding his arms around her back, arching her against him to plunder her sweet mouth. He'd just betrayed every archaeologist's rule, but his conscience was free. He'd done it for her. And he'd do it again.

That realization stunned him. He released Olivia and she looked up at him, questions sparkling in her eyes.

"Come on. We both could use a bath." He smiled, unable to resist stroking her dusty cheek with his fingertips.

"A bath! Where?"

Her simple joy made him laugh, soft and low. "I'll show you."

Often overlooked because it was so small, the Doclea Oasis belonged only to them tonight. Set on an endless plain of light-colored limestone rock, its northern perimeter was defined by date, olive and citrus trees. Soft grass grew along the bank of the spring where lemons and limes scented the air.

"This water's above blood temperature. How about a pitch-dark wallow under the desert stars?" he teased, putting behind them forever the overwhelming weight of Akim's madness and death.

Without a word, she peeled off the ruined linen as he stripped off his own clothes. The darkness cocooned them in a world all their own.

The imprint of her body had been branded on his soul from that first night in her room at the Winter Palace. Now as she stood, her eyes inviting, desire roared through him in powerful waves.

A wicked sexy smile curled her mouth. He reached for her, needing to touch her. Laughing, she backed away.

"Last one in buys breakfast!"

The perfect temperature of the water lapped at his thighs and stomach as he waded in after her. Again he reached for her and this time she sank against him, turning her mouth to meet his lips. Her long thick hair fell around them, closing him in a world of erotic sensations. He bit at her earlobe and tasted her lips again and again. Trailing kisses down her throat, onto her breasts to lick at their rosy tips, he lost track of his breathing.

He'd known it from the first moment. This woman was his forever.

"Olivia, love..." He stopped himself, closing his eyes in frustration. First, he had to convince her there were definite strings attached to his lovemaking, after all.

He opened his eyes to find her gazing at him in a way that made his body grow hard and hot.

"Say it again," she whispered.

"Olivia, my love. Always." His pulse beating like a bass drum in his neck, he picked her up in his arms, holding her tight against him, knowing he'd never let her go.

The grass felt soft and springy against Olivia's back and thighs where Ford laid her down. Content, she waited and watched him drop onto the ground beside her. His skin was hot and wet against hers.

His sweet voice murmured, "Olivia... Olivia..."

Whispering it again and again, pulling her mouth to his, he kissed her into a different kind of madness. If he didn't make love to her, she'd die. Yet, even knowing that, she tore her mouth away. Breathing heavily, she cupped his face and stared into his eyes.

"Do you know what it meant to me when you used that priceless gold hand to save my life? And when you allowed me to bury the mummy's hand in the desert?" she said.

The slow secret smile that had drawn her to him from the first curled his mouth so irresistibly, she nearly gave in. Instead, she arched away, searching his face.

"Do you know?" she asked again.

"I know I'm not as good an archaeologist as I thought I was. There was no contest. I'll always choose you above everything, Olivia."

While she could still think coherently, she asked the question burning in her mind. "It's only right that Charlie gets the glory of his find. But what about Akim?"

The moonlight turned his eyes a silvery blue. "We'll report him missing. Lost during the earthquake that destroyed the burial chamber. By the time we unearth that chamber and open the mummy case, there will be nothing left. It will be better that way for the government and for his friends and family."

Olivia knew she wasn't the same woman who had come to Egypt. "Now I can understand the Osiris legend—the love Isis must have felt for him. The kind of love poor Akim had for his wife."

Slowly, she moved her fingers to his mouth and he caught them, sucking gently.

"I didn't realize I could feel a bond like that with anyone. It's different than what Charlie and I experience. So different." Her heart pounded against her ribs at Ford's smile. Bravely, she plunged on. "I'm a compulsive 'neat Nelly,' you know. I'm going to clean up that dreadful office of yours. And I'm sure your perfect secretary and I will never see eye to eye on anything. I'll *never* understand why you like to spend your time in holes in the ground. From this moment on, I'm claustrophobic. And..."

He stopped her, brushing his mouth against her throat. His hands danced across the sensitized skin of her breasts and hips and up to capture her face.

"Once, I thought only the pyramids and the bits and pieces of the past I've found could last forever. Now I know there's something else."

She kissed his bare shoulder, looking beyond him to the endless sand meeting the fathomless black sky. Remembering the golden hand and the smaller, more precious one, she smiled. Yes, some things would last for eternity.

MILLION DOLLAR SWEEPSTAKES (III)

No purchase necessary. To enter, follow the directions published. Method of entry may vary. For eligibility, entries must be received no later than March 31, 1996. No liability is assumed for printing errors, lost, late or misdirected entries. Odds of winning are determined by the number of eligible entries distributed and received. Prizewinners will be determined no later than June 30, 1996.

Sweepstakes open to residents of the U.S. (except Puerto Rico), Canada, Europe and Taiwan who are 18 years of age or older. All applicable laws and regulations apply. Sweepstakes offer void wherever prohibited by law. Values of all prizes are in U.S. currency. This sweepstakes is presented by Torstar Corp., its subsidiaries and affiliates, in conjunction with book, merchandise and/or product offerings. For a copy of the Official Rules send a self-addressed, stamped envelope (WA residents need not affix return postage) to: MILLION DOLLAR SWEEPSTAKES (III) Rules, P.O. Box 4573, Blair, NE 68009, USA.

EXTRA BONUS PRIZE DRAWING

No purchase necessary. The Extra Bonus Prize will be awarded in a random drawing to be conducted no later than 5/30/96 from among all entries received. To qualify, entries must be received by 3/31/96 and comply with published directions. Drawing open to residents of the U.S. (except Puerto Rico), Canada, Europe and Taiwan who are 18 years of age or older. All applicable laws and regulations apply; offer void wherever prohibited by law. Odds of winning are dependent upon number of eligibile entries received. Prize is valued in U.S. currency. The offer is presented by Torstar Corp., its subsidiaries and affiliates in conjunction with book, merchandise and/or product offering. For a copy of the Official Rules governing this sweepstakes, send a self-addressed, stamped envelope (WA residents need not affix return postage) to: Extra Bonus Prize Drawing Rules, P.O. Box 4590, Blair, NE 68009, USA.

SWP-H794

HARLEQUIN®

INTRIGUE®

Harlequin Intrigue invites you to celebrate a decade of danger and desire....

It's a year of celebration for Harlequin Intrigue, as we commemorate ten years of bringing you the best in romantic suspense. Stories in which you can expect the unexpected... Stories with heart-stopping suspense and heart-stirring romance... Stories that walk the fine line between danger and desire...

Throughout the coming months, you can expect some special surprises by some of your favorite Intrigue authors. Look for the specially marked "Decade of Danger and Desire" books for valuable proofs-of-purchase to redeem for a free gift!

HARLEQUIN INTRIGUE
Not the same old story!

DDD